Once again Igor Malcev tried to reassure himself.
Goldman had probably decided to get himself
some medicine after all. It must have been truly
depressing to attend an important meeting with
dodgy bowels. He glanced at his watch and felt his
body give way to another fit of cold shivers. It was
almost eleven-thirty. The professor had been
absent for over half an hour. His previous
consternation returned – only stronger now.

Malcev bolted down the wide staircase and
hurried out to the pharmacy. No, they had not
served anyone this morning who answered
Goldman's description.

In another local pharmacy the answer was the
same.

Close to desperation, the captain returned to
the Academy. His last hope collapsed. Goldman
had not returned.

Wild alternatives flooded his mind. A chance
accident . . . hit by a car . . . sudden heart attack
. . . Goldman had a heart condition.
Accumulated stress could have triggered it.

Taken to hospital. Kidnapped by the CIA.
Fled to West Berlin. *Defected*.

*By George Robert Elford
and published by New English Library:*

DEVIL'S GUARD
KIZILKAR
THE SONNEBERG RUN

The Sonneberg Run

George Robert Elford

NEW ENGLISH LIBRARY

A New English Library Original Publication, 1986

First NEL Paperback Edition May 1986

NEL Books are published by
New English Library,
Mill Road, Dunton Green,
Sevenoaks, Kent.
Editorial office: 47 Bedford Square, London WC1B 3DP.

Typeset by Rowland Phototypesetting Ltd,
Bury St Edmunds, Suffolk

Printed in Great Britain by
Richard Clay (The Chaucer Press) Ltd,
Bungay, Suffolk

British Library C.I.P.

Elford, George Robert
   The Sonneberg run.
   I. Title
   823'.914[F]   PR6055.L

   ISBN 0 450 05908 1

For Andrea, Eldila, Georgina,
Robert and Edward Elford

Florence, Italy
1985

PROLOGUE

THE DERELICT coal mine ran beneath the Iron Curtain, that bleak borderland where the frontiers of freedom and slavery converged at a barrier of steel and fire. Stretching the length of Germany are barbed wire fences, minefields and constantly manned watchtowers. The mine, situated just outside the small town of Sonneberg, fifty-odd miles north of Nuremberg, had been a major working during the war when every ounce of coal under the earth was needed to fuel the Nazi machine. Some of its ancient galleries extended right into West Germany; the crumbling shafts at that end of the mine were perilous backdoors to freedom.

But communism does not tolerate backdoors to freedom, either on the ground or in the air – not even beneath the surface of the earth. With the erection of the Berlin Wall in August 1961, the mine had been shut down, its galleries and shafts systematically demolished, rendering them impassable.

A crack team of the Israeli Military Intelligence, among them a young woman and a former internee who had been a slaveworker in the mine during the last months of the Nazi epoch, dared to challenge the perils. They were to engineer the escape of a prominent Jewish scientist of Russian birth and get him safely to Israel. He was Jakov Abramovich Goldman, project leader on the guidance system of the SAM missiles the USSR manufactured in vast quantities and generously supplied to the Arab world.

1

IT WAS an ideal smugglers' night, warm and moonless, with just enough breeze to obliterate the sound of footsteps. The richly forested hills towards the border loomed dark and silent, fringed with tall, tangled shrubs and random boulders between which the narrow muletrack wound its devious path. Three miles to the north, the sparse lights of a small Turkish hamlet called Kilis challenged the un-broken velvet of the night. A short way to the south, the lamps of two Syrian villages sparkled, Azaz and Minnik, and just over the skyline spread the faint, milky haze of the distant town, Halep.

The four officers in the derelict hut had been waiting since dusk. Leaning against the wall, drinking the last of the rich, dark Turkish coffee, were Captain Adnan Ulutas and his second-in-command, Lieutenant Mahmud Sefke of the Turkish Security Force in the town of Gaziantep. Seated, wearing jeans, polo neck sweaters and leather flight jackets were Captain Hadar Harari and Lieutenant Jorv Amran of Shin Beth – the Israeli Military Intelligence.

The Turkish and Israeli officers had got to know each other during several previous joint ventures. Although neither the authorities in Ankara nor the elders in Jerusa-lem would willingly publicise the subject, Turkish and Israeli intelligence services had for years been collaborat-ing on matters of mutual interest. Such incidents were ample.

Together with selected Italian Red Brigade and West German Baader Meinhof extremists, Turkish terror commandos were regularly trained and equipped in Syrian-supported PLO bases which thrived under the protective triumvirate of Moscow, Damascus and Tripoli. Their principal aim was to subvert and destabilise NATO and pro-Israeli countries.

Due to their excellent undercover network in hostile lands, the Israelis were, most of the time, fairly well informed of imminent terrorist designs. Whenever they came across something important to the Turkish Government, the information would be relayed to Jerusalem without delay.

At the relatively young age of 32, Hadar Harari had already been promoted to the rank of *seren* – captain; he was a *sabra*, a native, born in Israel only a few hours after the historic Declaration of the Jewish State on 14 May, 1948. Harari's French-born parents had been among the few Jews who had somehow survived the Nazi deportation. In 1946 they had emigrated to Palestine, then still under British rule, using their French passports to land legally as pilgrims to the Holy Land. They stayed for the rest of their lives.

Fascinated by history and archaeology since his childhood, at 18 Hadar won a place at the Hebrew University in Jerusalem, only to suspend his studies a few days later to participate in the Six Day War. His courage and determination soon landed him in a special commando group of sixty crack soldiers, assigned only to beyond-the-front-line duties, far into enemy territory. Back in Jerusalem, he took part in the short, bloody battle for the Damascus Gate. His platoon had fought its way along El Wad and on to the Wailing Wall in the old Jewish Quarter. Three weeks after the battle, Hadar was once again back at the university, calmly studying archaeology.

Twice wounded in the Yom Kippur War in 1971, he was eventually promoted to lieutenant. Leading a team of commandos he was first to get across the Suez Canal and into Egypt proper. For this act of bravery he received his third decoration, and a promotion to captain.

Suntanned, tall and ruggedly handsome, with short blond hair and deep blue eyes full of vitality, Harari looked more Nordic than Jewish. He was an ardent chess player, a non-smoker, a rare drinker, and not particularly religious. He disliked traditionalism and the entrenched attitudes of his elders. Commando-trained, he was expert at judo and could handle most weapons with deadly accuracy. He was fond of fast cars and motorcycles, spending most of his savings on his obsession. He had lost his young wife, Laila, in a vicious PLO attack on a crowded supermarket four years before. It was this tragedy that finally induced him to join Shin Beth and fight terrorism.

Four years younger than Harari, Jorv Amran was a *segen* – lieutenant. Amran had been a fighter pilot in the Yom Kippur War. He had joined Shin Beth to fly special reconnaissance missions, carrying out the same sort of jobs Gary Powers had been doing for the CIA in the 1960s. He had been born in the United States of mixed American-German parentage and, apart from Hebrew, Yiddish and Arabic, he could speak English and German fluently.

In July 1976, Amran had been part of the Entebbe raid team; the bold *coup-de-main* that had liberated 103 hostages seized by Arab and German terrorists, fostered by the Ugandan dictator, Idi Amin. Then, in March 1978, during the brief Israeli invasion of Southern Lebanon, he had assisted in screening prisoners, which led Shin Beth to discover a vast quantity of concealed Soviet weapons. They had also been able to abort a scheduled PLO attack against an industrial complex outside Haifa, close to where Amran's parents lived. His only brother, David, had gone down with the submarine *Dakar* in 1968.

Only 5'6" tall, with a stocky, muscular frame, Jorv Amran was the happy-go-lucky kind; quick-witted and jocular, although his humour often skirted the fringes of sarcasm to the discomfort of all around him. With his curly dark hair and lustrous brown eyes, he could have passed for a

Latin. Indeed, by nature he *was* a Latin, being a passionate dancer, a good singer and a relentless chaser of women.

He was radical in his views and quite capable of offering an instant solution to all political, economical and military ills relating to the Middle East. It was his firm conviction that in the next bout with the Arabs, the Israeli Army should go all out to win, instead of halting and scurrying back at the first whistle from the United Nations, like a good dog.

Amran's martial outbursts were regularly aimed at Harari, but because he was more experienced and less volatile, the latter would simply display interest and gently manoeuvre the talk away from the thorniest subjects. In this way the two friends got along well; in Harari's opinion, Amran's views could be condensed into two Latin words voiced by the Romans over two thousand years ago: '*Recipe ferrum*' – Receive the Iron.

Jorv Amran loved adventure and was always ready for any precarious caper Shin Beth could think up exclusively for his pleasure. Under the command of Captain Harari, he had been to Turkey four times, and had come to like the country and its people. Warriors by nature, fierce and uncompromising fighters in combat, the Turks too seemed immensely impressed by Israeli military successes. Although Moslems, the majority of them had little sympathy for those Arabs who had been in the not too distant past subjects of the Ottoman Empire. Treacherous subjects who, by siding with the British and the French, had stabbed the Empire in the back and assisted in its downfall. Consequently, whenever the Israelis came back, they received a friendly welcome.

Captain Adnan Ulutas of the Turkish Security Force lowered his field glasses. 'All you can see over there was ours not so long ago,' he remarked, a catch of nostalgia in his voice. 'Everything belonged to Turkey, all the way down to Saudi Arabia.'

6

His Israeli colleagues nodded in sympathy. 'We would be happy to see you running things all the way to Saudi Arabia once again,' Jorv stated.

Harari knew his impulsive companion was not jesting; Amran meant it.

'Except, of course, for Israel,' Captain Ulutas commented good-naturedly, giving Jorv a friendly slap on the back.

Harari cut in with a smile. 'Yes, it's the one chunk of real estate we need for ourselves.'

The Turkish officer laughed. Then Ulutas's second-in-command, Lieutenant Sefke, said with emphasis, 'your bit of "real estate" has been expanding lately. New acquisitions left and right.'

The subalterns present broke into soft, respectful laughter and Sefke's eyes danced with amusement.

Captain Harari opened his hands. 'It was the penalty for being truculent,' he said, smiling innocently. 'Our Arab neighbours refused to negotiate. They preferred to fight.'

'They lost the battle, then they ran to the United Nations crying murder because you dared to follow their retreating armies,' said Captain Ulutas.

'That's right,' Amran agreed. 'Besides, who can see a border in the desert? Tanks and lorries can churn up a helluva lot of dust, you know.'

Harari took over. 'Lately it's become the fashion to demand land through claims based on ancient history. The PLO wants Palestine. The Armenians want Eastern Turkey because there had once been an Armenian kingdom back in the days of Emperor Augustus. The Polisario rebels claim Morocco. Argentina wants the Falklands. SWAPO wants Namibia, Khomeini the Persian Gulf.'

'You have forgotten Turkey,' Ulutas remarked amusedly. 'We grabbed half of Cyprus.'

'It was the wrong choice,' Jorv quipped, drawing instant frowns. Ever sensitive over the issue, the Turks had completed missed Amran's humorous undertone.

'Why was it wrong?' Lieutenant Sefke queried edgily.

The American-born Israeli answered bluntly. 'Because you should have seized the Middle East instead. Or at least Syria. And knowing how your army can fight, it would have taken you precisely two days to do it.'

This last comment went down well with the Turks. Their frowns promptly dissolved into benevolent grins as the officers laughed.

Amran's chin lifted. 'What is there to laugh about?' he asked with pretended dismay. 'Does that sound stupid to you?'

'No, not stupid. Not stupid at all,' Ulutas responded.

'Well, restoring at least some of the Ottoman Empire would have been the quickest solution to most of your local problems, including our much-desired safe frontiers for Israel.'

Captain Ulutas and Lieutenant Sefke were delighted by Amran's instant solution to an old malady.

'You almost gave us a chance back in '77, when you seized the Golans and advanced on Damascus. The Syrian Army was in a shambles. You could have taken their capital city. Why did you stop?'

Thinking that the Turkish captain was only joking, Harari answered his question in the same spirit. 'We didn't stop because of lack of fuel or ammunition. We lost Damascus and the opportunity for some sort of peace with Syria exactly where the West always has been and always will be losing: in the United Nations. Where – backed by the entire communist world – the Arabs can always raise hell. I'm sure you are aware of this. All those special General Assembly gatherings; all those threats of yet another oil embargo. Those are what prevent any progress.'

'Crap,' Amran spat the word. 'Even our closest friends were yelling their heads off: "stop the fighting!" Only while the Israeli Army was advancing, of course. When the Arabs are on the move nobody says a bloody word. Fine friends and allies we have.'

'Allies do not necessarily make good friends. Alliances are forged by fear, not by love,' Ulutas said serenely.

'True,' Harari agreed. 'And that's why we were not permitted to take Damascus and thus crush Syria once and for all.'

'A pity,' Ulutas commented wryly. 'If you had done, Syria would have disintegrated and we could then have moved in and reclaimed the northern half of the country with the port of Latakia, an ancient Turkish town.'

'Crammed with Soviet shipping and "advisers",' Amran blurted with baffled eyes. 'Are you joking?'

'Joking?' The Turkish captain looked deadly serious. 'Not at all, my friends. When you occupied the city of Quneitra and kept on rolling north, we were under the strong impression that Syria would soon be up for grabs. We were all ready to move ourselves. We had two hundred thousand troops and six hundred tanks on constant alert on the Syrian border. You should have advanced another thirty miles. That would have been enough.'

Still staring incredulously, Lieutenant Amran blew a soft whistle. 'Well, all this is news to me.'

'Naturally, we could not publicise the plan in the *Hürriyet*,' Captain Ulutas explained.

Harari, himself astonished, cut in. 'The Arabs would have cut off all your oil supplies.'

Ulutas shook his head. 'Not Iraq, though. Baghdad has been very reasonable since we built those dams across the Tigris and the Euphrates to regulate the flow of water across the border. We pay them for oil; they pay us for water. There are no price increases either. Iraq needs our water a great deal more than we need their oil. One can neither irrigate with, nor drink oil . . . However, if it is any consolation to you, the United Nations and our NATO allies are giving us similar treatment regarding Cyprus. The bloody Greeks are always right, the damned Turks always wrong. We tried to negotiate the issue for years. In the end we lost patience and moved in to put the house in order.'

'*Masallah, cok iyi yapmistiniz,*' Jorv delivered his

prompt support in Turkish. 'Thank God, you did it very well.'

At that Ulutas asked laughingly, 'You don't like the Greeks?'

'I have nothing against them, except that I'm disgusted by the way they're licking the oily Arab arse at Israel's expense.'

'They're only trying to safeguard their trade interests,' Harari interposed, at which the Turkish captain added, 'the Greeks are traders; we are warriors.'

There was a brief pause, before Amran remarked with ire, 'in the end, though, it is the Russians who constantly infiltrate and subvert. The USSR has an ideology; we have none. We have only improvised plans and haphazard actions. The Russians have long-range designs. For the time being they only realise these with little pinpricks; acts of terrorism in the free world, revolutions, little wars . . . no direct confrontation with the great democracies. Marxism is a powerful weapon.' Amran's voice dropped. 'The Russians use their doctrines on millions of halfwits all over the world. Now they have stooges armed to the teeth and ready to go on the rampage at Moscow's slightest bidding.'

Such as that very night.

Having completed a period of intensive training in sabotage and armed insurgency in a PLO camp near Homs, twelve members of the extremist Marxist organisation, Dev Sol, were about to re-enter Turkey in secret. Having learned about the project through an efficient spy network some time before, the Israelis had advised the Turkish authorities in Ankara, and now the local security forces were ready to receive them, with Harari and Amran in the team.

Spreading out along some one hundred yards either side of the trail, the troops lay in ambush. A couple of spotters using Motorola radiophones had been deployed a few hundred paces from the actual frontier line. Cavus Bekir, the sergeant in charge, carried an American nightscope, giving out an infra-red beam strong enough for him to spot a hare in the dark at two hundred yards. Since dusk he had twice seen Syrian border guards stroll past them, a good fifty yards inside Turkish territory. But, obeying his orders, he had let them pass unchallenged. Often the Syrians would intrude to test Turkish alertness before giving the green light to their clandestine wards to advance. Such violations were common events along the rugged frontier. As Necdet Turgutlu, the commanding colonel of the local security forces had jokingly put it: 'We cannot capture them all. If we did, half Assad's army would be sitting in Turkish jails, leaving no room for our own rubbish.'

But there had been armed clashes too, with casualties on both sides, whenever the Syrians or their Soviet sponsors wanted to test Turkish readiness in a sensitive region.

'In the past, they used to send up anchored observation balloons fitted with automatic cameras,' Captain Ulutas explained. 'Not lately, though. We used their balloons for target practice. Shot them all down, and they don't come cheap.'

The Israelis laughed.

Shortly after midnight, Cavus Bekir reported that a Syrian patrol had halted near his position and that one of their officers was giving the Turkish side a thorough survey.

'Probably trying to find out if it's safe enough for the Devcis to cross the border,' Ulutas explained. He then ordered the sergeant to stay low and to leave the Syrians alone.

Heavy with expectation, the minutes ticked by. With his elbows resting on a grassy ridge, Lieutenant Mahmud Sefke panned his field glasses along the mule track and up on the hillside, until it curved behind a cluster of ruddy cliffs. Eventually he let the glasses drop to his chest and gave a vexed sigh. 'Our illegal immigrants are overdue.'

Ulutas shifted his gaze towards him. 'When it comes to useful intelligence, our Israeli friends seldom err,' giving Harari a complimentary smile.

Turning to Sefke, the Israeli captain said with conviction, 'don't worry. Your wayward compatriots will show up before long.'

Sefke's reaction was a short, derisive snort of dismay. 'Compatriots?' He sneered and spat on the earth. 'The Devcis are Marxist-Leninists in Soviet pay. They have no God, no country, and are no compatriots to any honest Turk.'

'I'm sorry, I meant no offence,' Harari apologised. 'We all have our fair share of Russian-inspired trash.'

'Not that the Russians would ever lift a finger to help their stooges when they get into trouble,' Captain Ulutas took over in a voice taut with sarcasm. 'Back in '76, we caught four top Marxists, all fully trained in industrial sabotage, political subversion and espionage at a KGB establishment near Voroniez. Guilty of every imaginable crime, including murder. We tried the bastards and sentenced them to death. But, to give them their due, throughout the trial they behaved like convinced, hardcore communists. You know the sort of thing: lots of chest-beating about Marxism. Praising the USSR – where their allegiance belonged. When he sentenced them, the judge made a provision of clemency. He advised the four to contact the Soviet Embassy in Ankara and apply for entry visas to the USSR. "If the Russians grant you visas, you shall be permitted to leave Turkey and live in the country you now swear is yours," the judge told them. Ulutas uttered a soft chuckle. 'Needless to say, the applications were politely turned down in Moscow and the four devoted communists went to the gallows.'

'Moscow would never admit that KGB-trained terrorists had been sent to Turkey, or indeed to any NATO country. Nor would they ever allow unruly elements back into the USSR,' Harari commented. 'As far as the Kremlin is concerned, foreign-based left-wing extremists are little

12

more than deviationist trash, useful only as long as they are able to cause trouble outside the Iron Curtain.'

'Well, this lot won't be causing any more trouble – except perhaps to the Devil in Hell,' Lieutenant Sefke blurted.

'You are lucky,' Jorv said to Sefke, who frowned.

'Why lucky?'

'Because you can hang your killers and get rid of them for ever.'

Captain Ulutas pursed his lips. 'We have tried clemency in the past, but it did not work. It only created a vicious circle. Our soldiers captured terrorists, the martial judge sentenced them to hang, or go to jail for twenty years; then we restored democracy and the next civilian government freed them all. A few weeks later the bandits were back on the streets, more trigger-happy than ever, and the army had to step in once again. After the 1972 military takeover the army purged the country of terrorists and even of common bandits. In barely eight months we sent nearly forty thousand delinquents behind bars. Then the so-called democracy was restored. The socialist government of Bulent Ecevit gave them all amnesty. Immediately the street shootings, kidnappings, bombings and robberies began again. Twenty to fifty people a day were being killed in the violence. The army was compelled to act to safeguard the continuity of Turkey as a free nation. Apart from a dozen left- and right-wing terrorist groups, we also had a local Ayatollah who openly agitated against all modern institutions and wanted to push Turkey back into medieval times – the bey Erbakan, you might remember.'

'Yes, we know of your Necdet Erbakan,' Harari said. 'Islamic law. Three or more wives to each man. Breaking relations with Israel. Out of the NATO and avoid the Common Market. Back to the old ways.'

'Left, right, backward – we put them all behind bars,' Ulutas went on. 'But this time General Evren made sure that the terrorist killers weren't going into jail laughing and whistling the *Internationale*. And no lily-livered doves are going to bring them back into business either.'

Amran snorted with resignation. 'Unfortunately, we cannot do the same in Israel.'

Their conversation was interrupted by a call from Sergeant Bekir.

'*Geliyorlar yüzbasim*. They are coming!' Captain Ulutas announced tersely, then turned to speak into the Motorola radiophone. 'How many are they?'

'Twelve men.'

'You know how to proceed?'

'Yes, sir.'

Ulutas shouldered the radiophone and turned back to the Israelis. 'Let's go.'

Followed by Captain Ulutas's aide, Sergeant Yahyali, two non-commissioned officers and the Israelis, Ulutas and Lieutenant Sefke hurried over to a cluster of boulders near the trail, crouching as they ran. The Motorola beeped again. 'Their guide is passing us now,' Cavus Bekir reported in a low voice.

'Let him pass, then cut the line.'

'*Evet, efendim.*'

Nodding at the Israelis the captain said, 'you are now going to see a clever trick of theirs. About a hundred yards ahead of the terrorists there is a guide, probably just a common smuggler, trailing a nylon line, the other end of which is held by the foremost Devci. The aim is that if the guide runs into our borderguard, he jerks the line. It's a signal to the others that something's gone wrong and they should either scatter or turn back. The guide then gets a couple of months in jail for smuggling ten cartons of cigarettes or a few Japanese watches, or whatever he happens to be carrying.'

Harari nodded knowingly. 'So you let him walk on until all the others are in the bag.'

'Precisely.'

The wind stilled and immediately the air felt a little warmer. From the silent shrubbery emerged a soft, regular pat-pat, the tread of an animal. A solitary shape on mule-back materialised in the darkness and trotted leisurely downhill.

The guide.

Sergeant Bekir's voice crackled softly on the Motorola. 'The line has been cut, sir.'

'All right. You can stop him now.'

The guide was quickly blocked and taken into custody. He was a small, round-faced, beetle-browed peasant in his early fifties. Flanked by a pair of stoney-faced guards, he stood sullen and dejected before the officers. A long measure of line still dangled from his belt. Captain Ulutas flashed a thin pencil-beam into the peasant's face and his mouth widened in a broad grin of satisfaction.

'*Merhaba*, Hassan,' he greeted the prisoner in a jovially familiar tone, full of glee. 'This is old Hassan Keceli, from Kilis,' he explained for the benefit of the others. 'An acquaintance, oh yes. In and out of prison for the past ten years.' He turned back to the guide. 'Well, what have you brought from Aleppo this time?'

Wringing his hands, shifting uncomfortably, the man could only answer in a choked voice. 'Just a few cigarettes, a little coffee and a few watches, *efendim*.'

Ulutas slapped him on the back in a friendly manner. 'No meat?'

'Meat, *efendim*?'

'I mean the sort of meat that walks on two legs.'

No response. Ulutas shook his head reprovingly. 'Hassan, Hassan. Don't tell me that you buggered yourself up in real trouble this time?' He picked up the loose line. 'What's this for – fishing?'

The prisoner stood, silently perspiring. He kept his eyes fixed on the ground at the captain's feet in an attitude of utter submission.

'Shall I frisk him, sir?' Sergeant Yahyali asked. Ulutas shook his head in refusal.

'It won't be necessary, Sergeant. Hassan Keceli won't be armed. He knows the rules. Simple smuggling gets him six months to a year in the clink. Concealed weapon, five to ten years . . .' He paused, observed the man for a while, then continued ominously, 'something between three to five years for aiding illegal trespassers. More, if the trespassers happen to be wanted criminals.'

Again he looked at the guide with a curiously mild expression. 'What's going to be your score, Hassan?'

The little man squirmed, clenched and unclenched his hands, but said nothing.

'Speak up,' Ulutas prompted him, still in a friendly tone. 'Surely you are not scared of going to jail? To someone like you it must be the same as going home.'

'*Dayaktan korkiyorum, efendim,*' came the hesitant response. The officers laughed softly. 'He is afraid of being beaten,' Lieutenant Sefke explained to the Israelis.

Ulutas chuckled. 'Well, a little thrashing will do you good. For the benefit of your soul.' Speaking to Yahyali, he added, 'take him to the hut.'

Sergeant Yahyali's fingers clamped on the little smuggler's arm like a vice, making him wince. 'You're hurting me, *efendim*,' he complained. The commando sergeant chuckled and spat. 'You'll be hurt a great deal more when we get down to business.'

Half led, half pushed, the prisoner was taken to the hut and put under guard. 'Are you really going to thrash him?' Harari asked Sefke. 'He can't be important.'

The Turkish lieutenant opened his arms and grinned. 'It goes with our re-education programme. You see, we must convince the local smugglers that bringing in a few cigarettes is one thing, but helping the enemy is quite another. Men like Hassan don't care a fig for going to prison. They only fear the period between the arrest and coming before the judge.'

'Shh,' Ulutas hissed, silencing them as a cluster of dark shapes emerged into the open.

The twelve terrorists advanced slowly, turning left and right, constantly on the alert for trouble. They were still following the line which Sergeant Bekir had gathered in a

16

tight grip. Unsuspectingly, they walked straight into the circle of guns. A dozen torchlights lit up, transfixing the trespassers.

'*Dur!*' the sergeant challenged them. 'Halt!' He fired a short burst overhead from his machine pistol for emphasis. An immediate response came in the form of a loud curse.

'*Allah kahretsin, askerler!* – God damn it, soldiers!' The shapes dropped into the tall grass and vanished from sight, but a dozen salvoes coming from every direction convinced the group of the hopeless situation. 'Don't shoot! We surrender!' a voice called out in the gloom. 'Who wants to be shot for a few lousy cigarettes?'

'Come forward with your hands up,' Captain Ulutas commanded. The group of haggard men clambered to their feet. The soldiers quickly surrounded and frisked them.

The unexpected anticlimax made Harari purse his lips.

'The PLO would have tried to fight their way out,' he said with contempt. Ulutas turned to him. 'The terrorists seldom carry arms. Invariably they try to pass themselves off as common smugglers. But then, their guns and explosives are probably already here in Turkey, brought in by TIR lorries from Bulgaria and Czechoslovakia. Or even from Syria. There is a huge traffic between Sofia and the Arab countries via Turkey. We cannot dismantle and reassemble every vehicle. If we did the Bulgarians would do the same thing to our trucks hauling perishable stuff to Europe. They've done it before, delaying our lorries laden with fruit for days until the goods are no longer marketable.'

Sergeant Yahyali, who had directed the frisking of the prisoners, had found only Kent cigarettes, digital watches, bags of coffee and a few gold coins.

'No weapons at all?' Jorv Amran wondered.

'Not even a pocket knife.'

'They seem to know the rules.'

'It won't help them much,' Captain Ulutas commented grimly. 'We know very well who they are.'

The guide from Kilis and the twelve terrorists, now

17

sullen but orderly, were loaded into a waiting van and driven to the Security headquarters in Gaziantep.

Harari and Amran were summoned to the first interrogation interview. They entered a barren room at the headquarters, and saw the prisoners chained together on two long benches facing a table. Seated opposite them were Ulutas, Sefke and a hard-faced civilian who did not look up when the two Israelis came in. Ulutas waved them to a couple of vacant chairs at the back of the room, then resumed his place and continued a low-voiced discussion with Sefke and the civilian. Every so often, when Ulutas pointed out a detail or compared one paper with another from various folders ranged in front of him on the table, the civilian would whisper something, then look in the direction of one particular prisoner and nod knowingly. The muffled conversation was unnerving for some of the prisoners, who all remained very quiet.

Captain Harari studied their faces, feeling all the while that somehow he had already encountered them in Israel, in the Ghaza, in Samaria on the West Bank or in the army detention camps. For all their outward appearance these Turkish terrorists could well have been PLO, Al Fatah, or even paid assassins from Libya. His searching eyes encountered expressions which spoke of a wide range of human emotions: blind hatred, defiance, dejection, truculence. He saw also fear. They were all young men, most in their early twenties, none older than thirty. All moustached. Three of them were bearded in the fashion of Che Guevara – the worldwide trademark of Marxist agitators. Nervous hands fingered the strands, or dabbed at eyebrows and perspiring foreheads. Consternation. The silence was that of a tomb.

At a gesture from Captain Ulutas, Sergeant Yahyali walked up and down between the benches, handing out sheets of lined paper and pencils. 'Start writing,' he ordered gruffly. 'Name, date, place of birth, father's name,

18

mother's name, family status and home address, education, profession – when you weren't out killing people. The date you left Turkey. Where and what you were doing abroad, and try to make it plausible, gentlemen,' Lieutenant Sefke added in a minatory undertone. 'Otherwise there will be a short trip down to the basement. We keep the confessionals down there, just like the Christians in their churches. Except, in this building, there is no God. The Almighty is permanently absent. Keep it in mind. Screaming "Oh, God," "God help me," or "Allah, Allah" won't be any help.'

A hesitant voice rose up from the sullen group. '*Efendim*, we only went to Syria to buy a few cigarettes.'

Sefke cut him off in a tone that was deceptively mild. 'We know all that. It's your Number One cover story. You crank it out like an old record. Well, you'd better begin at Number Two. It'll save time.'

'*Efendim, Allahin askina* – for the love of God, sir.'

'Get writing,' Sefke snapped. 'Didn't I just tell you that Allah is permanently absent from this building? Later on you'll have more than enough time to recite the Koran.'

Twenty minutes passed. Still whispering over the outspread files and notes, the officers waited patiently. Jorv Amran noticed that the majority of the prisoners were writing slowly and laboriously.

'These lads might be dab hands at chucking grenades and shooting up villages, but when it comes to reading and writing, they're definitely in the elementary class,' he whispered to Hadar.

'Very true,' he replied. 'But then, the communist fighting machine doesn't need good minds to do its dirty work. Uneducated peasants are easier to keep in line.'

A grim-faced and ominously tranquil Cavus Bekir collected up the completed sheets and handed them to Captain Ulutas. They scanned all the papers, murmuring between themselves.

'Which is you is Ahmed Demirci?' Ulutas asked. There was a tense pause until a lean, gaunt fellow rose. He had shallow eyes set deep in a wedge-shaped face that tapered to a sharp chin. Like the others, he had a straggly moustache. 'I am Demirci,' he spoke, mopping his forehead.

Ulutas's lower lip curled down. 'Born in Ayvalik, 1957?'

'Yes.'

'Father's name?'

'*Evet, efendim,*' came the delayed response.

His voice was unconvincing. Harari knew the boy was lying through his teeth. Ulutas knew it too. He looked at the prisoner's mulish face, and suddenly ejaculated a sound of bitter amusement. 'We know, you lying scum, that your name is not Demirci. It is Sipahioglu.' Blood drained from the prisoner's face, leaving him white and sweaty. He swallowed and stood gazing at Ulutas like one who had been hit over the head.

'You are mistaken, sir,' he muttered at length. He was about to say something else when the captain's fist crashed on the table like a hammer on an anvil.

'Don't lie to me! Your name is Ali Sipahioglu, born Izmir on 5 November, 1955. Arrested four times for theft, robbery, distributing banned literature and political violence. You escaped from prison in Eskisehir.' He glanced up from the file he was holding and added with sarcasm, 'you have taken a long road home, but home you came. Short or long, the fugitive's way always leads back to prison, so you may as well drop this Ahmed Demirci stuff and confess. We have your fingerprints on file. All we have to do now is to take another set and compare them.'

'I want a lawyer, sir,' came the sullen response. 'All persons under arrest have the right to consult a lawyer. I am innocent. I want justice!' Sipahioglu emerged from his downcast mood and looked defiant.

Ulutas observed him levelly. 'We aren't the police, or the courts. If you are ever lucky enough to get before a judge, you can have a lawyer then. Sit down.'

'I protest —'

Sergeant Yahyali strode over and pushed him down onto

20

the bench, '*Domuza bak*. Look at the pig. If you don't shut your mouth you'll need a surgeon, not a lawyer.'

Another file. Another name. Another chained prisoner shuffled to his feet. He had a sulky, round face, thinning hair, a scruffy moustache and large, dark eyes – the left one twitched spasmodically, giving his face an incongruously lewd expression.

'Mustafa Yildirim,' Captain Ulutas read from the file with mocking emphasis. 'Also known as Bicakci. Also known as Sefik Reza. Hmm – two years at the University in Istanbul. You are a Dev Genc activist. Our records show that you have been involved in acts of sabotage, armed robbery. There are four murders against you. Among your victims was a customs officer. He left behind a wife and three children. A fine record for a student of philosophy.' He looked up. 'If you want to cheat the hangman you're going to need the best lawyer money can buy. But of course that won't be a problem for you, with half a million looted from the Akbank in Denizli. Have you still got it, or did you hand it over to the Palestinians?'

'Sir, I was not involved . . .'

'Shut up,' the captain cut him short. 'We are only getting better acquainted. The interrogation will come later, but not here. Downstairs. OK, sit down.'

Ulutas muttered a few words to Murat and the two men compared notes.

'More names, more lies,' he spoke aloud. 'Who is Aykut Yalvar?'

Another young man clambered up. Obviously terrified, he stood shivering and sick-eyed under Ulutas's cold gaze. 'The last time we caught you, your name was Ufuk Tasdelen, or am I mistaken? Aykut Yalvar, alias Ahmed Corbaci, alias Necdet Yargic. And so on with the rest of you Ahmeds, Mehmets, Mustafas.' The captain stood up, looking down on the prisoners with a menacing air. 'Now. I'm going to give you all a clean sheet of paper to try again. This is your last chance to tell the truth. You see, we know exactly who you are, so from now on just concentrate on the facts. Your mission, your destination, the names of your associates, the locations of your safe houses, the locations of ammunition dumps, all that kind of information. We don't care whether you belong to Dev Sol, Dev Yol, or Dev Genc, but you'd better get it right this time.'

At that moment another civilian came into the room. He spoke briefly to Ulutas, whose face lit up. Rising briskly, he beckoned his fellow officers and the Israelis into an adjacent office. A coded message and its translation lay on a glass-topped table.

NECOSM KURSASOK DYR YESOVA SNEV. MAFEK
TAB PAMAD 24-50-K30 IST ADRENE GTR. GP2
PILHAZYA BARUN. OMR SAMS DS FILTAB 8 HS.

'We found it hidden inside one of the prisoner's shoes,' Captain Ulutas explained, addressing Harari and Amran. 'Thanks to your collaboration on this project, we're going to get them this time. Please read the transcript.'

The English translation of the deciphered message ran:

Necati Osman Kurtulus, Savas Street, Diyarbakir,
Last house. Take 24 automatic rifles, 50
pistols and 30 kilos explosives to the Istanbul
address. The second group must prepare
the plan. Omer Samsun. Dev Sol. PLO camp
8 Homs.

'My congratulations,' Harari said admiringly. 'It seems you've got all the information you wanted. You certainly broke this one quickly.'

'It's a very amateurish code,' Ulutas said. 'Our expert had it deciphered in less than twenty minutes. But your help has been of immense value to us. All those weapons and explosives would have caused immense damage, not to mention the loss of life involved. And we would have had a whole gang of terrorists holed up in Diyarbakir. If it weren't for these arrests, they could have stayed on for months and none of us would have been any the wiser. As it is, we'll root them out before they can make trouble. The least guilty of them deserves to hang, but the leaders deserve to be hanged in every township from Istanbul to Kayseri.'

The house named in the coded message in Diyarbakir was an old, massive, two-storey stone mansion. As soon as they arrived, the security forces rapidly encircled it, trapping some forty terrorists inside. In the cold dawn light, the siege began. The insurgents were armed with automatic weapons and all manner of explosive devices, a veritable arsenal in a suburban home. The moment Harari saw the site he understood the seriousness of the situation. The Devcis had certainly selected their stronghold well. The building stood solidly on its own in the centre of a walled courtyard, but there were several other houses nearby, ordinary dwellings filled with families, thus ruling out the possibility of an aerial bombing, or even artillery shelling which – under more favourable circumstances – the Turkish Army would have carried out without batting an eyelid.

Deep-set, narrow windows gave the terrorists excellent firing positions, and whenever the troops moved out in the open they would unleash a hail of slugs and grenades at them in a display of defiant force. For the time being the commandos concentrated on keeping the enemy inside their compound, while the local police gradually evacuated the inhabitants of the surrounding houses through backyards and gardens. The situation was delicate. The troops could not advance, and the terrorists could not escape without exposing themselves to murderous crossfire.

An hour passed, the early morning calm occasionally broken by an angry spit of machine gun fire. The authorities decided to act.

Taking a loudspeaker, Colonel Necdet Turgutlu, district

chief of security, challenged the terrorists to surrender. His appeal only drew vicious rifle fire. A couple of grenades were lobbed from an upper window and demolished a lorry, wounding two troopers.

'We've got some hard-core bandits in that rathole,' the colonel commented edgily. 'We know the names of some, and suspect the identity of others. At least a dozen have had death sentences handed down to them *in absentia*. They have nothing to lose now. They'll decide to go down fighting.'

'What do you intend to do, sir?' Harari asked.

The colonel made an indecisive gesture. 'We must consider all the possibilities. I've had to rule out direct assault because I hate the idea of letting a single one of my soldiers die or be maimed for this scum. But the regional Army commander is on his way here now. We'll see what he thinks of the situation.'

After another uneventful hour had passed, during which the sun grew hot in the sky, a brigadier-general arrived by helicopter and took charge of the operation. Shortly after his arrival came a disheartening wireless report: one of the prisoners had confessed that the group occupying the mansion possessed four-inch mortars and at least two bazookas armed with twenty-four shells. So, instead of dealing with light armaments, the security forces were facing a major campaign. Plans to overthrow the terrorists would have to be adjusted accordingly.

Occasional messages were yelled from the windows. The terrorists wanted to negotiate a truce, but instead of giving up they haughtily threatened to raise hell in the town with their mortars. 'If the troops move against us we'll flatten the city!' their leader shouted from a darkened room on the second floor. To underline his threat a single shell was lobbed at random, which fortunately landed in a vacant yard causing no injuries, but considerable panic.

'They mean business,' Jorv Amran glanced at Harari.

'PLO training. Very efficient,' he responded flatly.

A brief horse-trading session ensued, with both sides hollering conditions and threats across the square. The Devcis wanted nothing less than unhindered retreat to Syria.

Not even the brigadier-general could think up a quick solution. He took all the officers into his command van and consulted his superiors in Ankara.

Amran spoke curtly. 'If I were the general, I'd order temporary evacuation of all civilians within a one-mile radius, then I'd use phosgene.'

'The Turks don't manufacture poison gas,' Harari answered sharply. Then he relaxed. 'But I like these prompt solutions of yours. Why don't you tell the general?'

Captain Ulutas returned half an hour later, full of confidence. 'We've got a couple of tanks coming over,' he announced. 'They'll make short work of this lot.'

Harari's brows lifted slightly. He didn't think tanks would make much of an impression on the mansion. A bouncing shot would inevitably land in the city centre, with disastrous results. But when he voiced his scepticism, Ulutas only smiled and shook his head. 'The tanks are not going to bother to fire at that place.'

'What are they going to do, then?' Amran queried.

'Wait, and you will see,' Ulutas answered enigmatically.

'What about those two bazookas up there?' said Harari.

'We are going to set up a smoke screen.'

'It's quite windy now. The screen might not hold.'

The Turkish captain opened his hands. 'As God wills . . .'

Fair enough, Harari thought. His long experience of Moslem 'philosophy' regarding God's will had taught him that – one way or the other – it would resolve every problem. Naive but reassuring tenets were stuck on the windshields of local lorries and buses, and the drivers seemed to have immense faith in them, even when they took a blind curve at seventy miles an hour on the wrong side of the road.

For over two hours there was a boring and nerve-wracking stalemate. Since the army didn't move at all, the terrorists thought they had the situation under control. In the end the government would prefer to let them leave quietly and get out of Turkey rather than risk exposing the local inhabitants of Diyarbakir to heavy casualties.

Neither side moved nor fired.

Towards noon, when the sun was burning overhead, there came the deep, ominous rumble of heavy engines over the clatter of tracked wheels. The racket heralded the arrival of two massive armoured tanks. Instantly the site came alive. Orders were cracked in hard voices. The troops cheered and began lobbing smoke canisters into the yard. Soon the tanks had lumbered into sight. Using the radio, Colonel Turgutlu rasped his last instructions.

Gears shifted. Heavy engines whined. The tanks picked up speed and began to race down the street towards the courtyard containing the mansion. Still puzzled, Harari turned to Ulutas. 'What are they going to do? Shell the house from twenty yards?'

'No, they'll smash them!' Ulutas replied forcefully, and smash them was what he meant – literally.

The windows of the mansion erupted with automatic fire. Rifle shots and hand grenades exploded along the pavement, some bouncing off the armour of the foremost tank. Then came a capricious gust of wind and the rolling layer of smoke momentarily lifted. Two bazooka shells slammed into the leading tank. The first bounced off the heavy armour and went wild, spinning crazily until it smashed into a parked tractor, blowing it apart. The second projectile landed on the left track of the speeding tank and erupted with an ear-splitting bang. The caterpillar snapped, feeding itself into the air, causing the tank to spin around and stop. Ulutas swore. Then everyone's eyes fixed on the second tank, rushing onward, partly submerged by smoke. Approaching the ten-foot stone wall at the front of the house, it reversed its long gun, smashed through, crushing a flight of steps, and tore straight into the building, knocking down the entrance and a third of the front. The firing stopped abruptly. The Israelis heard wild shrieks and curses, then sixty tons of reinforced steel tank began to turn around in what once must have been a room, momentarily vanishing under a cascade of falling masonry. The vast machine spun on its own axis like a raving dinosaur. Then, emerging from a sea of smoke and dust, it reappeared in the open, shedding rafters, masonry, stones and crushed pieces of furniture. And mangled corpses.

Barely pausing, it drove through the entire building, now knocking down the rear wall and drawing more screams as the upper floors tilted, slipped and crashed down, sending up great clouds of dust. Out spilled crazed men, now only broken bodies, followed by weapons and crates of ammunition. A handful of battered, bewildered shapes tumbled into the yard with their arms in the air – in vain; they crumpled up and died in a shower of bullets. Orders were to exterminate, not to capture.

Clattering back on top of the ruins, the tank rolled back and forth, spinning around and around, pulverising stone and wood in an immense cacophony of destruction.

After some time it withdrew, leaving behind a twenty-foot pile of debris and utter silence. The turret-hatch was flung open and the helmeted head of an officer appeared, spitting dust.

'*Iste işimiz bitmistir,*' Colonel Turgutlu stated grimly. 'Our job is done.'

Jorv Amran looked at his watch and blew a short whistle.

'Six minutes,' he commented appreciatively. 'The Turks aren't playing patty-cake with the bad guys, that's for sure.'

'Why? Do you think we are?' Harari asked ironically. 'I seem to remember our army blasting out quite a few Arab houses in this way during the clean-up operations.'

'Not while there were people still inside, though.'

'Unless they happened to be PLO . . .'

Amran shrugged. 'I don't think of the PLO as people, but as kind of oversized bacteria.'

Captain Ulutas cut in. 'We feel the same about our terrorists.'

That same evening Colonel Turgutlu invited the Israelis to dinner at the officers' club in the headquarters at Gaziantep.

Turgutlu was a short, stocky, bull-necked man in his mid-fifties; a forceful character with heavy muscles rippling under his shirt. His aggressive, military bearing was softened just slightly by his amiable character and the mild look in his eyes. After an exchange of courtesies and compliments and, of course, the customary glasses of *raki*, a powerful aniseed aperitif, he gave Harari a sealed blue envelope addressed to his superior in Tel-Aviv.

'Headquarters in Ankara have authorised me to give you this. It is a dispatch we received through our embassy in Moscow. Major Pesach already knows what it is: a small compensation for your collaboration,' he added complacently. 'The terrorists we eliminated today were important elements. This affair has had repercussions in virtually every principal city. Terrorist cells everywhere are collapsing like castles of cards. Our enemies at home and abroad will take years to rebuild them.'

Accepting the dispatch, Captain Harari answered, 'we only tried to prove that Moslem-Jewish cooperation is possible, Colonel.'

'Why shouldn't it be? We all descend from Abraham.'

Hearing this, Amran began to like the Turks even more.

Colonel Turgutlu asked jovially, 'why don't you Israelis offer some sort of compensation to the Arabs? That would put an end to this business of constant warfare, which helps no one except Moscow.'

'How can we offer anything to people who don't even talk to us, sir?' Harari countered with a query of his own. 'The Arabs, especially those whose lands are safely far away from Israel, don't want peace. The further away they are, the louder they holler for blood. The PLO does not want peace. An end to hostilities would only cut off those hefty Saudi subsidies, a large chunk of which the top men regularly pocket. Nor would peace suit Moscow's designs in the region.'

The colonel shrugged. 'Then you should beat them down once and for all, and afterwards display benevolence. Magnanimity is the victor's privilege.'

Harari thought for a moment, then asked cynically, 'would the Soviets allow the utter defeat of their clients to take place, given the consequent loss of communist influence in the region?'

Colonel Turgutlu waved an impatient hand. 'The Soviets, the Soviets – the great, malicious shadow,' he said disgustedly. 'The entire world trembles over what the Russians might or might not do. The Russians no more want a large-scale war than they want a cholera outbreak. They want small, local ones that they can manage all right. But in a global war, in total war, they would have to face Armageddon just like the rest of us.'

At that moment the orderly served fresh glasses of the fragrant Altinbas Raki. Turgutlu lifted his glass. '*Serefe*,' he toasted the Israelis, and they drank.

'In the 1950s I was serving in the Kars district,' the colonel continued. 'Near the Soviet border. It was hell up there then: wire fences everywhere, mined fields and watchtowers at five-hundred-yard intervals. Ha! I remember some of the good times we had. The local Turkish commander used to exercise the troops by sending them across the border to steal the phone-relays – little grey boxes – attached to the towers. Anyone who got all the way over and snatched a box received three weeks' paid leave. Believe me, those soldiers would tunnel under the fences like bloody rabbits, remove the mines and steal the relays right from under the noses of the guards pacing on the platform overhead. Moscow sent protests which we put exactly where they usually put foreign complaints. The Russians only swore and put their bloody relays higher up on the pylons.'

The Israelis laughed. 'I can imagine their faces,' Harari said, and Turgutlu burst into renewed guffaws. 'Imagine their faces when their patrols strolled along the mined stretches with the position of a dozen mines altered!'

With that they all went in to dinner.

In the morning an army helicopter flew Harari and Amran to Adana airport where their sleek, unmarked Kfir TC7 trainer was parked under guard far out in the field.

Closing the canopy, Amran said, 'I am curious about what's in the blue envelope.' He nodded at the plump package, marked 'Highly Confidential', in Harari's hand.

Belting himself in, Harari replied with a chuckle, 'you needn't worry. Whatever it is, we are certain to be involved in it. It won't be an Israeli job, either.'

Giving the instrument panel a last check, Amran replied, 'as long as Pesach keeps us out of the USSR. Any idea what it could be?'

'Some,' Harari nodded. 'One thing I'm certain of is that any business Pesach may have in Moscow would have to involve prominent Jews. The Shin Beth wouldn't care a damn about anything else over there.'

'Oh yeah? What about a few Soviet weapons secrets?'

Harari shrugged. 'Aren't we getting all that from the Arabs free of charge?'

Permission for take-off came crackling through on the radio.

'Okay, here we go,' Amran announced cheerfully. He liked air travel, but only when he was at the controls. He grumbled constantly when he was forced to be a passenger, saying that he could sense every mistaken manoeuvre of the pilot, knowing every possible consequence and therefore worrying a lot. Out loud.

Their Turkish escort, including Captain Ulutas, saluted. The Kfir sped down the tarmac and lifted off, gaining altitude rapidly. Lieutenant Amran banked out towards the shimmering sea, taking a south-westerly course and passing Cyprus on the wrong side to keep a healthy distance from the Syrian coastline. Soon Turkey was behind them.

30

2

MAJOR MOSHE Pesach was jarred awake by the phone ringing loudly on the bedside table. Yawning and scratching his slightly balding head, he struggled into a kind of semi-wakefulness, turned on the reading lamp and reached for the receiver, quietly cursing the late-night caller. He had sat up working until well past midnight and now, glancing at his watch, he realised it was barely daybreak. Only five-thirty, he grumbled to himself, now even more convinced that being in the army was a great deal worse than driving a cab or an ambulance.

'Pesach,' he grunted into the phone, but he brightened the instant he heard the sonorous contralto tones of a woman.

'Major Moshe Pesach?' she asked carefully, making sure that her call was being taken by the right person.

'As far as I know,' Pesach replied good-humouredly, already alert and fit for amusement. He was fond of women. In the hard, martial world in which he spent most of his time, pretty women with soft voices and gentle eyes constituted the bright sky.

'So, what makes a young woman call me at this unearthly hour?' he prompted her. The soft chuckle at the other end of the line pleased him.

'What makes you think that I am young, Major?' she responded spiritedly. Pesach felt content. He was playing the right tune.

'You sound it,' he stated matter-of-factly, then added for good measure, 'You are pretty, too.'

He heard a girlish giggle. Yes, she is pretty, he thought.

'For all you know, I am fifty years old and ugly,' she taunted gently.

'Prove it.'

More soft laughter. A brief pause. Then she said, 'I am putting you through to Colonel Achim.'

'There is no need to hurry.'

· 'Well, Major – this is an urgent service call.'

'Then you should tell me your name, rank and business,' Pesach responded in a tone of pretended authority.

'My name is Miriam.'

'A truly feminine way of reporting. Miriam what?'

'Sergeant Miriam Eskhol, sir.'

'That's better . . . Well, Sergeant Eskhol, the next time you call me, kindly do it around five in the afternoon, before I leave the office. Then we could have a drink together and get to know each other better.'

'I am sorry, sir, but we don't get schedules for urgent service calls.'

'It doesn't have to be a service call,' Pesach joked.

The door of the master bedroom opened. Pesach's wife, Esther, poked her face around the gap and asked sleepily, 'who is it at this hour?'

Pesach covered the mouthpiece. 'The army. Who else would it be at half past five in the morning?' Turning away from her, he continued over the line in a strict tone. 'Very well, Sergeant Eskhol. Put me through to Colonel Achim.'

He cupped his hand over the mouthpiece to speak to his wife just before she closed the door. 'This is why I prefer to sleep here, close to the phone . . . Sorry you woke up.'

She sighed. 'Don't worry, I'm used to it. If you must go somewhere now, Moshe, there's some coffee in the thermos flask.'

'Thanks.'

She closed the door. The telephone line crackled and

Pesach recognised the deep, throaty voice of the commander of the Bet Arif fighter base.

'Moshe, your people are back from Turkey,' Colonel Achim said without preliminaries. 'Our Ankara friends have sent you a sealed envelope marked urgent and confidential. It's waiting here at the office for you. Can you come in now and get it?'

'It is urgent, damned urgent.' Pesach was exultant. 'Thanks for the call, Yoel. Ask Harari and Amran to report to me immediately. No showers or coffee first.'

'At your place or in the office?'

'The office,' Pesach replied, groping for his trousers.

'They'll be there in about forty minutes. *Shalom*, Moshe.'

Pesach waited on the line for a few seconds; perhaps that Eskhol girl would come on again. Hearing nothing more, he replaced the receiver, resolved to take a look at Achim's new secretary one of these days. He hadn't really appreciated Selma, the previous one, who had hated office work and insisted on being relocated to the front where she could shoot at Arabs. But later he had discovered that she had good reason to be bloodthirsty. During a skirmish on the Golan Heights, Selma had fallen into Syrian hands. Her captivity had lasted for only three hours, but it had been enough time for her captors to rape her over and over. When at last the Israeli paratroops struck and the Syrians fled, the first thing Selma did was to grab a discarded rifle and shoot her fleeing abusers – between the legs. An expert markswoman, most of her slugs landed where she wanted them to land and condemned the three culprits to lifelong abstinence. She would have dealt the same treatment to the pair who had held her pinned down during the rape, but the commanding officer of the paras restrained her – the same Yoel Achim, then a major. Enraged and nearly hysterical, Selma fought him viciously, threatening to blast off his balls also. She ended up in a psychiatric ward for a brief spell of treatment, after which Achim had arranged for her transfer – to the air base. She went grudgingly, hating men in general and Arabs in particular. The doctors told Achim that she had been a virgin.

Pesach dressed quickly, his thoughts returning to the Ankara dispatch – a mission of the utmost importance. God bless the Turks. If all Moslems were like them, there'd be no problems in this part of the world.

He went into the kitchen and poured himself a hot coffee, appreciating Esther's attention. She was a good wife, if somewhat cool and formal. Still, Pesach felt rotten whenever he cheated on her. Still, it wasn't his fault that the bloody army was crammed with pretty women, most of them young and spirited; that he liked them all and couldn't bear to miss a chance. At the age of 46 he considered himself a man in his best years and luckily mother nature supported his claim with benevolence. Pesach was blessed with a noble, masculine face, a strong, authoritative character and a quick wit. The black patch he wore over his left eye, a memorial of an ugly wound that should have killed him, instantly reminded strangers of Moshe Dayan, the hero of the Six Day War.

Before leaving, he looked in on the children, asleep in their rooms – a habit he had acquired over the years. They were sound asleep. Two boys and a girl. The right combination. His youngest one, Yoel, had almost been killed the year before when his school bus ran over a PLO mine. Four children aged between six and twelve, as well as the driver, had died in the explosion. The goddamned terrorist way of fighting. Three of the culprits had been caught and Pesach had learned that the Arab commando unit had planted twelve more mines along the dirtroad to the Rosh Ha Ayin kibbutz, ten miles east of the city. He had called the local police to have the road closed immediately and, not wasting any time, drove the captive terrorists out to the site. He then made them walk along the road and recover their own mines. Eight Russian-made RPGs had been removed, the ninth blew up when one of the PLO team accidentally trod on it. The rest of the deadly devices were defused by Israeli experts. 'Bad luck,' the local chief of police had commented after the blast.

He took the Jeep from the garage and drove off on the ten-mile drive to the Shin Beth compound. Dawn was breaking, light clouds high in the opal sky promising beautiful weather.

As soon as he read the dispatch, he got back into the Jeep and took off straight for Jerusalem. Harari and Amran were left waiting in his office. These orders had to be cleared at the top first.

After Major Pesach had finished detailing his proposals for accomplishing the project outlined in the Ankara dispatch, he waited patiently for the Cabinet Minister to gather his thoughts before venturing a tentative, 'what do you think of it, sir?'

The cabinet minister did not answer immediately. Instead he rose and paced the lushly carpeted floor, apparently deep in thought. He stopped in front of the window and stood for a while, gazing down at the ancient walls of the old city and the brisk traffic. 'It is truly uplifting to be back in the capital,' he remarked after a while, as if speaking to himself. He returned to his desk, but did not sit down. Instead he planted his palms on the polished ebony surface in a slightly bent attitude and observed Pesach with mild curiosity, and perhaps a hint of sarcasm.

He spoke slowly, emphasising each word. 'Well,' he began, his crisp accent belying the heritage of his years in the British Army. 'Governments change, ministers come and go, but Moshe Pesach is going to be here forever.'

Major Pesach caught the double meaning of his name, which was the Hebrew word for Passover, one of the major feast days in the Jewish calendar. His brow lifted slightly in a querying expression, but he said nothing. Eventually the cabinet minister sat down and responded to Pesach's previous question.

'You asked me what I think of the matter?' he said

slowly. 'Well, to begin with, I cannot help but wonder why the Turkish Foreign Ministry should have sent you personally such an important dispatch, instead of observing the usual protocol and sending it to the Israeli Government through our ambassador in Ankara.'

Pesach's face was without expression. 'I don't think the Turkish Foreign Ministry has been involved at all, sir . . .'

'Oh, I see. It is strictly an army-to-army matter?'

Major Pesach nodded and grinned modestly. 'The quickest and safest way to move sensitive material, sir. It's very likely our Turkish friends didn't want to pass it through any intermediary hands for security reasons.'

'Perhaps, perhaps,' the minister commented. He observed Pesach's face for a while, then continued with a slight edge, 'you know, sometimes I get the impression that you espionage *chachomim* are turning Shin Beth into a sort of ultra-exclusive outfit, the members of which know a great deal more about what's going on than the Prime Minister himself.'

Major Pesach smiled complacently and permitted himself to repeat the minister's own words.

'As you have rightly asserted, sir – governments change, ministers come and go – and who knows where they might be going? Some information shouldn't go anywhere, but should stay right here with Shin Beth.'

At that the minister burst into laughter. 'Yes, yes. You lot don't have to contend with elections or changes of staff. All right, Pesach. Your team is truly ingenious. They've proved themselves again in Turkey. I'm quite ready to overlook this slight affront to protocol. Professor Goldman is very important to us. Bring him safely back to Israel. But, unless your derelict mine really *is* negotiable, your chances are no better than that of a penguin cast abroad in the Negev desert.'

For a while he sat in silence, studying the file. 'Ariel Cohen – a jeweller from Tel-Aviv,' he muttered aloud.

'With him acting as their guide, our team have a very

fair chance of success. Cohen knows the mine well,' Pesach cut in.

'I see he was a former deportee. He worked there . . .' He glanced up. 'This Cohen chap may know the mine the way it was, but not the way it is now.'

'We have already taken that into consideration, sir. According to our expert in Berlin, the blocking of the galleries has caused a certain amount of damage here and there which – given a little time – could be cleared by our team. They will be carrying enough provisions to last for one week underground. They intend to carry out this job in secret, not while under hot pursuit.'

'It may still happen – the pursuit.'

'Even so, the team will have adequate means to fend for themselves. It is not easy to follow armed fugitives in narrow galleries where only a few men may advance at one time. If the worst comes to the worst, they can blow up the passages behind them. That would give the Russians something to worry about.'

The cabinet minister considered this while Major Pesach continued to wait patiently.

'Have you already contacted this Mr Cohen?'

'Not yet, sir, but I have sent him an invitation to come and see me. I wanted to have your consent first for Project Sonneberg.'

The cabinet minister nodded his head and smiled ironically. 'My dear Major Pesach, I've been told that you've always managed to railroad people of your choice off to places you want them to be, but you cannot just enrol a 54-year-old jeweller – a family man – for such a perilous mission in a communist country.' He paused for an instant to study the file, then added, 'I see Mr Cohen has never been involved in any kind of direct action.'

'He's done his time in the army, so I am hoping he will volunteer.'

'It is a great responsibility . . .'

'We do have a very capable man already in East Berlin. He will be of great help in organising the actual snatch.'

'Yes, I know – Lieutenant Karlim. A brave fellow.'

'As I said, he managed to get into the mine recently, Pesach added emphatically.

'And he really does consider it negotiable?'

'Yes – at least down to the second level.'

The cabinet minister rose. Pesach followed suit.

'Keep me informed.'

'Do I have your assent to proceed with Project Sonneberg, sir?'

'You do. Get on with your crazy plan, and don't lose Goldman. You know I'm game to every gamble you concoct, Pesach. I remember well when you snatched that radar station from Egypt. Nevertheless, I will want to study the detailed plans before you set the project in motion.'

'Of course, sir.'

'If Captain Harari and Lieutenant Amran do return safely from East Germany with Professor Goldman, give them a promotion and a modest rise in pay.'

'It is already scheduled, sir.'

'Well – good luck.'

Whistling merrily during the sixty-mile drive home, Major Moshe Pesach felt elated. It was lucky that he had found the minister in good spirits. He was sure that Harari and Amran would carry the mission through to a successful conclusion.

Somehow.

Near the village of Ben Shemen he turned off the Jerusalem–Tel-Aviv highway and took the secondary road to Bet Arif to pay another visit on his old friend, Colonel Yoel Achim.

And, of course, to have a closer look at Sergeant Miriam Eskhol.

Colonel Sasha Gorin sat rigidly, glancing occasionally at light flurries of snow brushing at the high, arched windows, while his superior, KGB General Semion Sherbakov studied the rather thin file on Professor Jakov Abramovich Goldman. He read swiftly and intently, commenting every now and then as he scanned the different entries.

'Section 26 – foreign mail control, negative. Section 12 – foreign phone control, negative. No mail and no calls from abroad during the past five years. I see the secretary of the housing complex has provided a complete list of the individuals who were observed frequently visiting the professor's residence over the past three years. Some eighteen individuals. Mostly colleagues and party members. The District Party Secretary has endorsed them. So has the Academy of Science – although I dislike that remark, "without reservation", which is wrong. There are always reservations, for everyone.'

He moved a silver cigarette box across the desk and said without looking up, 'you may smoke if you wish, Comrade Gorin.'

The comrade colonel thanked his comrade general, and took a cigarette. He was careful not to blow the smoke across the general's desk. Sherbakov went on reciting aloud. 'No foreign visitors. No interviews with foreign pressmen. The professor's son, Oleg, is a lieutenant in the Army Agitprop in the Far East. Daughter, Olga, married to a project engineer in Tobolsk – party member for fifteen years. Regional Komsomol activist before . . .'

He lifted his face for the first time. 'Where is the report from the *Yevsekzia*?' he asked, shuffling the papers, looking for the notes always supplied by the KGB Jewish Office.

Colonel Gorin consulted the notes on his lap. 'Page eighteen, Comrade General,' he advised respectfully.

General Sherbakov scanned the indicated entry, nodding occasionally, obviously satisfied.

'No religious inclinations. Jakov Abramovich has attended synagogue services twice in the last four years. The marriage ceremony of a distant nephew and the funeral service of a deceased colleague. We may call those visits acts of common courtesy. I would have done the same . . .' He lifted his eyes and looked directly at Gorin. 'Professor Goldman appears to be leading an exemplary life as a Soviet citizen.'

'He was decorated twice for valorous conduct under enemy fire,' Colonel Gorin ventured. Now that his superior had voiced his opinion, he thought it expedient to put in a good word for Goldman.

'I have noticed it,' Sherbakov said with a nod. 'Decorated after the battle of Kursk and once again after Kishinev. And in 1960 he received the Order of Socialist Labour.'

With a resolute flick of his hand he snapped shut the file. Placing a palm on it, he asked, 'what do you think of our Professor Goldman, Comrade Gorin?'

'He is a Jew, but I think he can be trusted completely.'

The moment he said it he realised his mistake. General Sherbakov threw back his head and laughed.

'And there you are completely mistaken, Colonel Gorin – just like the Academy of Science. You must never allow your vigilance to sag. No one can ever be, as you say, trusted completely. There are of course citizens whom we may trust to a certain extent, and there are others less trustworthy; still others wholly untrustworthy. But no one merits our unconditional confidence.'

'If you say so, Comrade General,' Colonel Gorin responded with perceptible reluctance. The KGB general must have noticed the frown on the dark brow of his subordinate, for he concluded his observation with a corrective line: 'Outside the Kremlin and the Central Committee of the Party, naturally.'

Colonel Gorin wanted to steer the exchange into more cheerful waters.

'Not even you may be fully trusted, Comrade General?' he ventured a polite jest, which Sherbakov took good-naturedly.

'Sasha Petrovich, I can issue exit permits for others, but not for myself. You see, I don't qualify. Nor do you. There are too many confidential matters we know about.'

'I don't wish to go outside the Soviet Union anyway,' the colonel responded flatly. He said it with conviction, but still his superior tilted his head and threw him a candid glance, which Gorin didn't quite like.

'Come now, Colonel Gorin – we would all like to take a stroll on the other side; in London, in Paris, in Rome, to name a few places . . . Even in America. There's nothing wrong with that.' Then he added with mocking emphasis, 'if only to see for ourselves all the wrongs of capitalist society. Why should we deny it?'

His face creased into its habitual shark's smile and he chuckled. 'This building is about the only place in Moscow where one may talk openly about everything without infringing the law.'

The colonel wondered why Sherbakov was pushing him in this way. He stubbed out his cigarette and decided not to volunteer himself for any Beria-style game of subterfuge. So he answered even-voiced and in full accord with the official line.

'We know what's wrong with capitalist society without actually going there, do we not, Comrade General? One only has to read Marx and Lenin.'

'And *Pravda*,' Sherbakov added in the same even tone. But he had taken Gorin's response somewhat sourly. 'I am appalled by your decorum, Colonel. You have an impeccable record and I think I should nominate you for promotion . . . There is a top position vacant up in Kamchatka.'

Gorin stared at him for a moment. Sherbakov's ugly suggestion of a place 'a thousand miles behind God's back' – as the army used to refer to remote and hostile regions – was in very bad taste. He stiffened, opting for the standard answer to such offers. 'I am ready to serve my country anywhere.' But the idea lingered in his mind that for some obscure reason his superior was deliberately taunting him.

General Sherbakov's brows lifted a little and he looked at Gorin with an expression of commiseration.

'All of us are ready to serve our country anywhere, twenty-four hours a day,' he replied with a grin. 'I only tried not to be overly formal with you. We have known each other for a long time.'

'So we have, Comrade General.'

'Fifteen years . . .'

'You are very kind to remember so well,' Gorin said formally.

General Sherbakov rose, signalling the end of the meeting.

'Take the Goldman file and send the relevant papers to the passport office.'

'It will be done, Comrade General.'

He saluted stiffly and left the sumptuously furnished office with its padded doors.

When he left the cold, massive grey building – palatial yet tomblike – Colonel Gorin felt relieved. Leaving his private Lada in the car park, he decided to walk home, still pestered by a vague sensation of discomfort.

He was mystified; his mind invaded by question marks. Why should Sherbakov choose him of all people to play these vicious games with? For what reason? He tried hard to remember if he had failed in anything lately; in service, or in his private life. He could not recall blundering anywhere at any time. Not in the recent past, anyway. He had observed all the rules, bungled no jobs.

Then, why all those sudden question marks?

It occurred to him vaguely that such question marks belonged to everyday Soviet life. The life of every citizen was built upon question marks. When one of them could not be answered, the citizen's world crashed apart.

Colonel Gorin shuddered and quickly dismissed his heretical thoughts. Perhaps he was only imagining implications behind Sherbakov's taunting remarks, threats that did not really exist. KGB officers liked to play on the taut nerves of others, even if they did happen to be colleagues. It was part of their job. Even casual, wholly unfounded and unjustified stabs in the dark would sometimes 'make the rabbit jump' – as Beria used to say.

Suddenly he recalled a friendly game of chess he had once played with the dreaded security chief in the officers' club. Beria had been talking all the time, uttering double-edged remarks throughout the game. 'You made some good moves and achieved an excellent position with all its advantages,' he would say enigmatically after Gorin, then a young lieutenant, had moved a piece on the board. 'But, you see, sometimes even the best position becomes untenable . . . The apparently clever move fails and an important piece finds itself trapped. One should always move very, very carefully. It only takes one wrong move and – zap. Checkmate.'

That sort of ominous remark constituted Beria's favourite pastime. He loved to see his subjects nervous, concerned, feeling suspected of doing or saying something only God knows what. Beria had considered himself extremely witty when, summoning a subordinate, he had told him on the phone, 'come around in the evening, but first tell my secretary what you would like to eat for your last dinner.'

Gorin also recalled the case of an elderly major, an excellent chess player, who had taken the supreme chief's ominous remarks so much to heart that he had shot himself in the head the same evening. When Beria received the news, his only comment was a quiet, 'the unfortunate major must have had improper ideas in his head.'

Beria's ornery was well known. He used to play cat-and-mouse games with even his highest-ranking subordinates, especially with those about to be purged. No one felt safe in his presence, under the python-like gaze of his eyes behind the gold-rimmed pince-nez.

Perhaps General Sherbakov too had been playing chess with Beria and had decided to adopt his style.

And also his smile.

Still, these thoughts did nothing more than make him feel insecure. At least the comrade general had passed

43

Goldman's application. Gorin would have felt a bloody fool if he had been checkmated after making an airy promise that he could sort it out.

For the third time that morning Ariel Cohen read the brief, enigmatic summons. The address, he remembered vaguely, was that of some military establishment a few miles outside Tel-Aviv, on the highway to Herzliyya. He had driven past the place a few times without paying any attention to it. Now, straining his memory, he managed to conjure up the image of a double-fenced enclosure guarded by watchtowers, with a cluster of single-storey buildings, a fuel dump with barrels stacked high under camouflage netting and a similarly camouflaged motor pool of Jeeps, Dodge lorries and armoured troop carriers. A standard army establishment.

Ariel wondered what business the army could possibly have with him?

Department 4-B, Office 12. That told him nothing.

The owner of a small jewellery store and workshop, Ariel Cohen, aged 54, was a typical example of the prosperous, small Israeli businessman: correct, law-abiding and proud of his nation. His only previous encounters with the authorities had derived from parking tickets and income tax matters – and those only when he felt overcharged and filled reimbursement claims.

Born in Hungary, Cohen had emigrated to Israel – then called Palestine – shortly after the holocaust. He was of medium build, with dark hair and eyes, and fleshy lips. His lined forehead showed to the top of his skull where his hair had receded, and he had a hawk nose. Cohen was an Askenazim, who had returned to the promised land to enjoy the gift of human dignity in a country he could claim as his own. He had survived deportation to Nazi Germany, but had lost his entire family to the SS murder machine. After the liberation he did not feel like returning to Soviet-dominated Hungary, where the majority of die-hard fascists and traditional anti-Semites had simply divested their green Arrow Party shirts and donned red ones instead. In the Sonneberg mine he had worked with several Ukranians who convinced him that the Russians were only slightly less fanatic Jew-haters than the Nazis. Although Stalin did not use gas-chambers, he classified all Jews as class enemies which, according to communist terminology, equalled a protracted death sentence; a slow execution under inhumane conditions in rigorous labour camps located in the most hostile regions of the USSR, where Jews were permitted to perish together with all the other undesirable elements.

Without any racial prejudice, naturally, which did not exist in the Soviet Union.

At the time Cohen had expressed his astonishment about the scores of Jewish names in the upper Soviet echelons, but his fellow Ukranian deportees contemptuously told him: 'They are no longer Yids. Now they're Bolsheviks, with no more kind sentiments towards Jews than Himmler's.'

So, after the liberation, Ariel Cohen had fled to Vienna where he spent several weeks in the Rothschild Spital on the Waehringer Guertel, then a well-known staging centre for clandestine *aliyahs* – emigrés to Palestine. At length he arrived in the port of Taranto in Italy, where he boarded a derelict freighter bound for Haifa. But ill-luck still dogged his steps.

A dozen miles off the coveted Palestinian coast, a destroyer from the British Royal Navy had halted the transport. The passengers had been taken to a British KZ in Cyprus. Already well conditioned to the calamities of life, Ariel accepted this ironical twist of fate with patience. After all, there was no forced labour, no beating and torture in the British camp. 'You shouldn't lose heart,' he used to urge his fretting companions. 'We have survived under Hitler. Compared with the Nazi camps, this one here is a sanatorium. Just imagine you are on vacation after a long period of hardship.'

Nonetheless, when an unexpected chance presented itself, Cohen had fled. Some Tommies on duty began firing after him, but 'missed' all the time. After a brief odyssey in a tiny fishing boat, he had finally landed on the deserted Palestinian coast. But soon he bumped into a group of garrulous Arabs who stripped him of his meagre belongings, then drew lots over whether the *Yehudi* should be handed over to the British, or simply thrown back into the sea. Probably he was saved by the timely intervention of some armed men from the Stern Gang – a Zion extremist organisation which recruited him on the spot. Ariel did not mind fighting for the creation of a Jewish homeland, but the aims and methods of the group he soon learned to dislike. He had come to this land to find a new home and to live in peace. Never having been a particularly enterprising person, he refused to believe that terrorism could be the proper way to found a nation. He also thought it abhorrent to kill British soldiers, who only followed orders from London. Like the majority of Hungarians, he was a convinced Anglophile. Perhaps it had something to do with the early years of the war, when BBC newscasts had represented the only truth in a vast sea of Axis lies. It was also a faint ray of hope for the Jews who, after the capitulation of Italy, firmly believed that a British paratroop landing in Budapest was imminent. During the war, the word 'British' was synonymous with justice, uprightness, tenacity and liberation. He had grown up with such traditions and they had deep roots.

Perhaps the British had hampered Jewish settlement in the Mandate, and secretly sympathised with the Arabs, most probably for economic reasons. But the British contribution to saving the lives of those tens of thousands of Jews still languishing in Nazi camps towards the end of the war was immense. British sacrifices shortened the Hitler order and prevented the conclusion of the 'Final Solution' to the Jewish 'problem' in Europe. Always objective, Ariel Cohen also judged the matter from this angle.

He was unable to turn his gun against the British.

He had voiced his objections openly, and the Stern Gang had immediately dismissed him as unreliable. Then he joined a kibbutz near Gadish, in the Emeq Yizreel up in the north, and fought against armed intruders. After the birth of the Jewish State he became a soldier of the Haganah – the core of the Israeli Defence Force.

Returning to civilian life, he learned the goldsmith trade from an old Viennese jeweller he had befriended at the kibbutz. With the compensation received from the West German Government in 1954 he opened a workshop, later adding a jewellery store. He then met and married Sarah.

Cohen was not interested in politics and strifes now. Like most common people on receiving an invitation from the authorities which did not specify the reason, Ariel anxiously tried to guess what it was all about.

Why should they send the summons to the shop, instead of his home address?

His son!

The sudden paralysing thought froze the marrow in his bones. Shmuel was in active service. God forbid if anything had happened to him . . . Israeli parents with sons in the armed forces had to be forever prepared for sad communications.

Cohen dabbed his neck and forehead and went to fetch a cold beer from the fridge. He tried to convince himself not to worry. Shmuel was a pilot. If anything was wrong with him the note would have come from the Air Force.

'Maybe they've just got the wrong Ariel Cohen,' he told himself aloud. There were at least five other Cohens doing business along the Petah Tigwa. He wanted to call Sarah, but decided against it. Why worry her as well? He could tell her in the evening, or not at all. All the same, he phoned home to tell her not to expect him for lunch. He would be out of town for the afternoon, on business.

At precisely one o'clock he closed the shop and drove his battered little Fiat along Abba Hillel Avenue, past Hayarkon Park, across the river and out towards

Herzliyya; he wanted to take a closer look at the place he was to visit tomorrow.

Camp Bezalel. A roadside arrow pointed towards the unmarked wiremesh entrance guarded by a sentry box.

Acting on impulse, he stopped and walked up to the sentry.

'Shalom, Corporal.'

'Shalom, sir. Can I help you?'

'Yes. Could you tell me what sort of establishment this is?'

The astonished frown on the young soldier's face told him: Ari, you are an idiot.

'Have you ever been in the army, sir?' the sentry queried with disdain in his voice.

'Of course,' Cohen answered. 'I only asked because —'

'Then you ought to know that I cannot answer such questions. Please move on, sir. It is not permitted to stop here.'

'I have to report here tomorrow,' Cohen added hastily, and stuck the summons under the sentry's nose.

'You'll find the officer in charge here tomorrow morning, sir,' came the evasive response.

Cohen murmured his thanks and drove off.

The name Ytzhak Nahim rang a bell in his mind. A one-time compatriot, friend and client, Ytzhak had been working in the Ministry of Defence until his recent retirement. Of anyone, he should be able to tell him something about this enigmatic place and its Section 4-B . . .

He stopped at a bar in Ramat Gan, called Nahim, and told him briefly about the summons. After a pause Nahim explained to Ariel that he was not alone, and anyway he would prefer to talk to him in person. He would come to the bar.

Ariel ordered a round of chicken sandwiches and a mug of beer and sat down to wait, reading his copy of the daily *Haaretz*.

His friend arrived, and after getting a beer for himself and another for Ariel, scanned the summons. A minute

48

later he said in a casual voice, 'Section 4-B, Office 12. It's the Shin Beth set-up. Military Intelligence.' He looked at Ariel's baffled face, then added tauntingly, 'obviously they want to find out about something that you already know.'

'I haven't done anything wrong,' Cohen exclaimed, as confused as before. 'Are you kidding? As far as I'm concerned the Shin Beth should be looking out for Arab terrorists and protecting military secrets. How does a Tel-Aviv jeweller fit into the picture?'

Ytzhak smiled serenely. 'The Shin Beth has many jobs to do, Ariel. If I remember well, Office 12 has something to do with Eastern Europe.'

Cohen thought this over and his countenance brightened.

'They might want to know something about Hungary, or about certain Hungarians I might have known in the past . . . Yes, now it begins to make sense.'

'Perhaps,' Ytzhak replied meditatively. 'In any case, it can't be anything bad, Ari. Otherwise they would have sent a Jeep with escort for you, not an invitation.'

'I'll tell you all about it tomorrow.'

Ytzhak shook his head. 'Whatever you discuss with the Shin Beth chaps would better be kept strictly to yourself. They don't like talkative people.'

Two thousand miles away in Moscow, Professor Jakov Abramovich Goldman locked the door of his apartment and slumped down into the chair behind his desk.

Placing his newly-acquired passport in front of him, he gazed at it for a long time – incredulously and almost with reverence. He opened it with unsteady fingers, turning the pages, scrutinising the ornate seals and stamps, the exit permit, the official entries . . . everything appeared to be in perfect order. At long last the much-coveted miracle had taken place. All those years of psychological poker with the KGB and the Communist Party had finally paid a dividend. It was worthwhile being patient. His personal file at the dreaded secret police headquarters was now endorsed: AB-1.

A sacred designation, rare as a diamond. Given only to trustworthy government employees who might travel outside the USSR. His passport marked 'Non-diplomatic Government Service' entitled him to generous allowances while abroad and customs benefits upon returning.

But Jakov Abramovich Goldman knew that he wouldn't be coming back to Russia . . . Oh no. With God's help he would spend the rest of his life in Israel, in the service of his own people, free from constant fear and the grim, numbing self-discipline that governed the lives of Soviet citizens.

God bless the Israeli agent who – it must be eight years ago – had advised him against applying for a permit to emigrate to Israel, or, as a matter of fact, against setting foot in a foreign embassy, or in a synagogue, or participating in any Jewish gathering.

What was the agent's name? Moshe Pesach, that was it. If he had not followed his counsel he would have lost his job and become a marked man with no chance of ever leaving the USSR.

If he had not listened to Pesach, the best he could have hoped for would have been exile to Birobijan, the so-called Jewish Autonom Region in Far Eastern Siberia, near the Chinese border. He could also have been designated insane, and locked up in a psychiatric unit to be 'cured' of his erroneous ideas.

And of his will to live.

Abiding by the Israeli's words, Professor Goldman had lived the disciplined life of a devoted Soviet citizen and Communist Party member. He selected his acquaintances with meticulous care, rebuffed any with undesirable political leanings, and attended every important Party seminary and political gathering. Very occasionally he would voice a derogatory remark about America, the CIA, NATO, or Israel. Not too often and nothing too fanatic. Just a little

50

something to show where his 'loyalties' lay. When, four years before, the Academy of Science wanted to send him to a conference in Hanoi, he had politely declined the distinction, giving the irrefutable reason of having some unfinished experiments to conclude; missile guidance systems of great importance to the Red Army that could not be set aside, not even for ten days.

The generals constantly watching him had naturally supported him; Goldman had gained several positive marks on his record for that one.

He knew that sometimes the party and the KGB would test selected cadrés by apparently nominating them for foreign travel, especially to the richer capitalist countries. Invariably the trip would be cancelled at the last moment, the idea being to study the reaction of certain prominent citizens to the prospect of going abroad. Many of those who accepted the chance too eagerly ended up with low security ratings.

Professor Goldman, however, had been nominated for real. In just a few weeks, he would be on an aeroplane, flying away.

True enough, he would only travel in fellow communist countries, but there wasn't a country in the world as impregnable as the USSR, where no one could even approach the confines without being stopped and checked a dozen times. At any given point the frontier defences of the Soviet Union were at least fifty miles deep. To enter one needed special passes, visas, letters of invitation . . . documents and more documents. Even stricter restrictions applied to the immediate five-mile zone.

Now he felt relaxed. His itinerary detailing his 15-day visit to Bucharest, Belgrade, and lastly Dresden, then returning direct to Moscow, had been passed in secret to a certain person at the Turkish Embassy. Of course, Goldman would never be allowed to go near a Western embassy. Nor could he use the phone. He had been told to advise a fellow Jew, an insignificant tailor in a clothes factory who was permitted to work at home in his spare time, serving private clients. He had visited Samuel Efre-movich for the first time to order a couple of good suits for his forthcoming foreign trip, and had then carefully passed on to him a copy of his travelling schedule. Ten days later he received his new clothes, together with a brief message: 'You shall be met in East Berlin. The password: *Pesach.*' It appeared that Comrade Samuel Efremovich also happened to be making a suit for a low-ranking official at the Turkish Embassy.

All was ready. Behind him were the years of kow-towing to blunt-faced KGB officers – unintelligent thugs puffed up with self-importance. Ahead lay Israel, the land of the fathers.

He got up from his chair a trifle stiffly to pour himself a brandy. No more Russian winters to get through, either.

Since the death of his wife, Juliana, in 1975, Professor Goldman had lived alone. His daughter, Olga, had moved out to the east with her engineer husband; his son, Oleg, was a Red Army officer also stationed some two thousand miles away. Both were well settled and should be relatively safe. Anticipating his eventual defection, the professor had scaled down contact with all his friends so that lately his social relationships consisted of only a few letters of insignificant context. He hoped fervently that the KGB would realise their uninvolvement. In Stalin's time a similar defection would have caused the downfall of even distant friends, but now the Soviet system had changed somewhat for the better and it was no longer quite like the old joke went: 'There are three kinds of people in the USSR. Those who were in jail, those who are in jail, and those who will be in jail.'

He knew he would not be left alone on the trip. He was to have an 'assistant' – a certain Comrade Igor Malcev, who had already been introduced to him as an 'Intourist travel expert', ostensibly coming along to ensure the pro-fessor's comfort. He would be arranging transport, hotels, meals, meetings. Judging by his age, Professor Goldman thought, his helpful Igor should be a First Lieutenant in

52

the KGB. But he had underestimated his own importance. Malcev was already a captain, well-known to Western counter-intelligence services, including Shin Beth. No matter how carefully the escape mission was planned, the professor knew that Igor Malcev would have to be handled with extreme caution. He was clever and he was dangerous. A perfect KGB man.

Igor Malcev, immaculately turned out as always, presented himself at Goldman's apartment two days before their scheduled flight to Bucharest. He wanted to give a hand with the professor's suitcase; a last check-up, the elderly scholar commented to himself. Playing it safe, he had only packed clothes and a few scientific publications freely available in Moscow book stores. And when Malcev politely suggested that he might like to take along a few family photos, the professor declined, saying, 'what for? On a trip of only two weeks?'

From a precious carved wooden box that his parents had given him on his graduation, he took only an old golden pocket watch with chain, inherited from his father. He also packed eight gold roubles. 'We might want some entertainment, or souvenirs not covered by the official allowance. I hope it is not forbidden to take a few coins along?'

'Take them, by all means.' Captain Malcev was all benevolence. 'I am bringing a few myself.' He showed Goldman a small purse containing similar coins, only more of them. 'I want to buy a German tape-recorder.' He gave the professor a conspiratorial wink. 'A few grams of gold won't ruin our economy!'

Jakov Abramovich Goldman had also ensured that his escort would see his modest stock of jewellery, mostly that of his late wife, had been left locked away in his desk drawer. He hoped that this gesture would dispel any lingering doubt about his bona-fide intentions. The KGB was a vast warehouse of lingering doubts which could never be wholly dissipated. People intending to defect, however, would invariably try to rescue at least their easily portable assets – such as jewellery.

He wanted to sustain the psychological game until he was safely with the Israelis.

Apparently Igor Malcev was satisfied with Goldman's preparations. Nevertheless, he took charge of the locked suitcase to dispatch it to the airport. 'This way, we won't waste any time checking through customs,' he explained helpfully. 'My own luggage is there already.'

Fair enough, Professor Goldman mused. Luggage already checked by the KGB won't be opened again by customs. The divulgence of the good KGB captain was so transparent that he could have laughed openly.

Although Malcev did not ask for them, Goldman also gave him the keys to his cases, even though he was certain that the secret police possessed keys to every lock in the world, perhaps even to the gate of paradise.

When he was alone once again, he wondered how the Israelis intended to ferry him over the West German border? Personally, he could not envisage any easy way. The Israelis were aware of his age and condition, and surely would arrange their plans accordingly. He had great confidence in the ability of the team from Tel-Aviv described to him in detail by the Turkish official via his tailor. He would never have considered an escape with any other Western organisation. Had the CIA been waiting for him in East Berlin, the New York dailies would probably have been headlining his defection before he managed to leave Moscow Airport. The British Intelligence virtually crawled with KGB plants and the West German BND people could not even dine with a Russian citizen without an East German STASI snooper looking over their shoulders.

With the Israelis it was different. The very character of the Jewish State excluded, or at least vastly minimised, hostile infiltration. Jews might quarrel among themselves, but they would never betray their country. Goldman was convinced that the KGB had eyes everywhere, except in

Israel. A Russian Jew sent to Israel would probably defect the moment he set foot in the country!

The necessity of leaving behind all his possessions, among them a collection of rare books, slowly acquired over the years, saddened him, but he accepted the sacrifice philosophically. Human freedom and dignity never came cheap; especially not freedom and dignity for a Soviet citizen.

Except for occasional palpitations and slightly elevated blood pressure, he considered himself physically fit. During the last year he had been conditioning himself by taking long walks, and doing some jogging and gymnastic exercises. Still, he hoped he would not be taken on a long trek through woods and muddy fields or swamps, which was how he imagined illegal border crossings to be.

But why had not the Israelis chosen Bucharest? Ceaucescu's regime was much milder than Hoenecker's. Romania was closer to Israel . . . There were also the Black Sea and the Turkish coast to aid a quick getaway.

The Israelis probably had good reasons, however, for choosing East Germany.

3

Major Moshe Pesach received Ariel Cohen with a strong, warm handshake and a broad smile, offered him a comfortable club chair and sat down himself in an adjacent one instead of behind his desk, emphasising the informal nature of their meeting. Major Pesach seemed very different from what Ariel had always thought an intelligence officer would be like. His host was a jovial, friendly man in his early forties, perhaps a little on the plump side with a black patch over his left eye that reminded Cohen of General Dayan.

He soon learned that Moshe Pesach was a man of tactful reasoning and subtle persuasion. Ariel Cohen had no way of knowing that he was sitting next to one of Israel's most efficient 'headhunters', as the former SS General Eichmann could well have testified. Major Pesach had played a major part in the historic capture of the Nazi, and had assisted in scores of other daring enterprises.

Judging from the piles of folders and files on his desk, the *Aluf* must have been a very busy person. Moments after Cohen sat down, a pretty WAC sergeant with long, fair braids and slender legs entered, carrying an armload of files, looking at Pesach questioningly. The major pointed at the only vacant spot on his desk; she placed her load there, gave the two men a charming smile and left the office.

'Isn't she a pretty creature?' Pesach asked in a familiar tone.

'Is she your assistant?' Ariel asked, to which Pesach

replied sourly, 'Unfortunately not, but my last ambition in life is to take her to bed.'

He said this as if he and Ariel had been close friends for years. Completely at ease now, Ariel decided that he had liked the intelligence chief from the moment they shook hands.

Rolling his eyes and waving a futile hand, the major went on, 'But it's no go. She is the daughter of my general – probably still a virgin. Between ourselves we call him Daddy King Xerxes.' He drew the edge of his palm across his throat. 'Such is life.'

He lit a handsome Dunhill pipe, watched for a moment the smoke curl towards the open window, then, looking closely at Ariel with his solitary but intense eye, he said in a quiet, balanced voice, 'I invited you to come and see me because we need your help, Mr Cohen.'

'My help?' he exclaimed. 'Do you want me to estimate the value of some jewellery?'

Pesach joined Ariel with a soft laugh of his own.

'Unfortunately we aren't wealthy enough to possess any gold. Shin Beth is run on a tight budget. No, we need your help to prepare for a very important mission. An assignment that must be carried out very soon. Abroad.'

He reached for a yellow folder on his desk, opened it and scanned the first entry. Ariel got a glimpse of the heading. 'Project Sonneberg', and instantly confused thoughts flooded his mind. The Shin Beth must have caught another Nazi war criminal, he thought, perhaps the commander of the mine, and they want me to testify.

After a moment's silence, Pesach said, 'I understand you spent the last seven months of your deportation in the Sonneberg coal mine, now in East Germany.'

'A subsidiary of the Dresden-Heidenau steel works . . . Yes, I was there,' Cohen answered, though still puzzled. 'It was run by the SS.'

The major's eye transfixed him.

'Do you remember the place well?' he asked warily. 'I mean, after so many years . . .'

Ariel uttered a bitter chuckle. 'Sonneberg was not a place to forget easily, Major,' he replied wryly. 'Himmler made sure that we should remember.'

Pesach elucidated. 'I am asking you about it in the technical sense, Mr Cohen. Whether you remember in detail the layout of the mine?'

Cohen considered this for a moment. 'Yes, I should think so. I do believe I could walk along those accursed galleries blindfold. Even today, thirty-five years later.'

'Very good.' Pesach's good eye twinkled with interest.

His remark left Ariel wondering what on earth could be so good about Sonneberg? He came to the conclusion that it could not be the case of some captured Nazi. But what other significance could that Godforsaken place possibly have for Shin Beth?

'Could you tell me the nature of your interest in Sonneberg, Major Pesach?'

The major considered for a moment, then, leaning over, he tapped Ariel on the knee. 'The mine might serve us in the near future as a relatively safe escape route for some important Jews presently living behind the Iron Curtain.'

Cohen's eyes lit up with interest.

'A brilliant idea, Major . . . Yes, it should be possible. Come to think of it, the complex must be situated on the border. Several galleries should have exits on the West German side . . .' He rose exulted, and walked over to the large map of Central Europe on the wall. 'With your permission . . .'

'Please.'

Ariel studied the map.

'Sonneberg is not shown on this plan, but it should be right here, opposite Coburg.'

'That's right.' The intelligence chief knew the location of the mine without looking.

Ariel returned to his seat.

'Whom do you want to help escape, Major Pesach?'

'A Jewish scientist. A very important one.'

'I didn't know there were any prominent Jews left in East Germany.'

'The scientist we have in mind is a Russian.'

'A Russian Jew? God. Then he really does deserve a helping hand. If I can be of any assistance in your mission, Major, I am at your disposal.'

'I'm very happy to know that, Mr Cohen,' Pesach replied emphatically.

There was a short silence while Pesach refilled his pipe; then Cohen spoke. 'One thing still strikes me as odd. The East German communists are doing their utmost to contain their reluctant people behind walls, fences and minefields. Why should they leave open a backdoor to freedom? They must know all about Sonneberg, and they seem to have thought of everything else, as far as I know.'

'They have,' Pesach responded. 'The mine was shut down twenty years ago. At the time they destroyed the galleries leading to West Germany. They were systematically razed on every level, rendering them impassable.'

'But there are eight levels at Sonneberg. The fourth, fifth and sixth have several excavated galleries in the direction of Coburg. I'm certain no one could blast anything on level six.'

'Why not?' Pesach asked eagerly.

'Because of the occasional methane leaks. Workers down there carried facemasks and used only copper tools. Picks, rails, the wheels of the coal cars and even the hobnails of the SS boots were made of copper to prevent sparks.'

All attention now, Pesach was scribbling notes. His chin came up. He observed Cohen for a while.

'You were barely eighteen then, yet you remember it all so well. Amazing.' He leaned back and crossed his legs. 'Mr Cohen, we have reason to believe that under certain conditions the Sonneberg mine is still negotiable. The communists did not manage to demolish it completely.'

'It would have been impossible. Some of those galleries

are a mile long. Others run directly under the water basins and cannot be tampered with.'

'Precisely,' the major agreed, 'and your knowledge of the mine could be of invaluable help to us.'

'But, Major, I have no idea of the present state of the mine.'

'I have,' Pesach countered firmly. 'You see, we have a man in East Germany who has already surveyed the upper galleries.'

'He's gone inside?'

'Down to the second level.'

'How? Without the elevator working . . .'

'By using a special winch which he thoughtfully left in position for future use. He spent two days down in the mine. I understand he has already cleared some debris.'

Cohen nodded his head in silent appraisal.

'He must be a real daredevil, Major.'

'He is indeed,' Pesach conceded with a fatherly smile. 'Our Lieutenant Karlim. In Berlin, of course, he lives under another name.'

'Until now it has never occurred to me that communist Germany could be of any interest to Israel,' Ariel confessed. 'At least, not to the extent of keeping an agent there.'

Major Pesach was amused.

'East Germany is a very important Soviet warehouse for shunting military hardware all over the world, including the Middle East for the PLO. So far, the West German Government does not sell weapons to Arab countries – that would be immoral. German weapons should not kill any more Jews. But no similar moral principles are applied to East Germany, whose official history begins after 1945, with the Nazi past conveniently eliminated.'

'Major Pesach, how did you come across my name?' Cohen asked quietly.

Pesach chuckled. 'Have you forgotten the curriculum vitae you wrote for the *Irgun Zvai Leumi*?'

'What curriculum vitae?'

'Soon after you landed in Palestine.'

Cohen tapped his forehead twice. 'Oh, yes. I remember now.'

'Also your subsequent conversation with someone called Eli Moos?'

'One of the Stern leaders. Yes, now I remember him; an inquisitive man.'

'He had to be.' Pesach tapped the folder in his lap. 'It's all here.'

'Don't say . . .'

'Naturally we keep files on every homecomer to Eretz. Studying those files is part of my job. We also have considerable data on all former Nazi establishments, including Sonneberg.'

He knocked the sticky debris from his pipe and cast a long, level look at Ariel. 'Surely you remember the name, Martin Drexler?'

'The SS engineer – *Hauptsturmführer* Drexler? But he was no more SS than myself, Major. Drexler helped us all to survive. He was a saint, in his way. I hope he was not sent to jail after the war?'

'No, no,' Pesach replied reassuringly. 'He was a fine German who wore the SS uniform only because he had to. We know that. He was never put on trial for anything. Even the Association of Jewish Deportees testified on his behalf. Yes, Drexler is still alive, now an old man in his seventies – partly paralysed these days.'

'I'm sorry to hear it,' Ariel said with genuine sadness. For a moment his mind wandered into the realm of old memories. Martin Drexler, the only kind German among a bunch of oafs who had smuggled in extra loaves of bread, sometimes meat, the odd sausage and a bit of honey for his pitmen – as he used to call the deportees. An SS officer who demanded proper clothes, footwear and safety equipment for the Jews. Constantly he would remind the commandant of the mine: 'The Führer expects us to supply our war industry with coal, but I cannot increase production with invalids, or half-dead labourers.' And when

61

the *Obersturmbahnführer* reassured him that the SS could supply three fresh Jews for every dead one, Martin Drexler rebuffed him boldly with a derisive, 'trained pitmen?'

There had been a few other decent Germans as well. Like the elderly peasant woman who had tossed a sackful of potatoes into the Jewish column on the march to Sonneberg, for which she received a vicious blow over the back from the guards. By the time the SS had searched all the prisoners for the 'illegal ration', everything had been devoured, peel and all.

Ariel was glad to hear that Martin Drexler was alive. 'I will write to him,' he said resolutely, and was surprised to see the major shaking his head. 'You should not write anything. I'll explain why not presently.'

Then Cohen asked, 'Major, how have you come to know Drexler so well?'

'Because he has been helping us.'

Ariel stared blankly. 'You mean, recently?'

'Until his stroke, two years ago. There are quite a number of Iron Curtain Jews in Israel, thanks to Herr Drexler. He had also been helping Simon Wiesenthal in Vienna.'

'The Nazi hunter?'

'That's right. And he never asked for anything in exchange. He said he wanted to atone for at least a tiny fragment of the holocaust.'

The conversation lapsed for a while. Pesach began shuffling his papers and Ariel waited patiently.

Pesach continued questioning him about the mine, and asked Cohen if he remembered many details, however insignificant they might seem, because the smallest point could turn out to be of the utmost importance. Ariel replied ponderously, straining through the foggy mists of half a lifetime.

'I can even tell you how long it takes to walk from Pit No. 3 on Level Three to Toolshed Five on Level Four. It is exactly eight hundred and seventy-two paces.'

'My compliments.'

'Not merited. I counted those steps twice a day for seven months.'

'Do you think you could help us to work out the safest way to the West German side?'

'We would need a detailed groundplan to do it.'

'We have a groundplan. A copy of the original drawn by Martin Drexler.'

'Then we should have no problem.'

Pesach rose. 'Would you like a cold beer, Mr Cohen? Or may I call you Ariel?'

Pleasantly caught by surprise, Cohen replied civilly, 'of course – certainly. My friends call me Ari . . . A beer would be fine for me.'

'In turn just call me Moshe, as my friends do,' Pesach suggested. Ariel was delighted. After all, it wasn't every day one got the chance to become friendly with intelligence chiefs. Ariel remembered the old days, back in Europe. He had only ever encountered stoney-faced, sour men. Gestapo-like. Yet Pesach acted like an old acquaintance – a sympathetic fellow.

On Pesach's part, however, it had been a subtle manoeuvre to relax Ariel Cohen before coming to the crucial part of their conversation.

From a small fridge he brought two cans of Israeli beer and handed one to Ariel, together with a plastic cup. For a while the two men sat in silence, sipping beer, then Pesach asked another question. 'How about your health, Ariel? I mean, your physical being . . .'

The unexpected query caught Cohen by surprise. 'My – physical condition?'

'That's right. How do you feel, generally?'

'Fine, I suppose – at least so far,' he said with a baffled look. 'Why?'

'No serious complaints?'

'Indigestion.'

'We all get that,' Pesach commented. 'Are you active? Do you take some sort of exercise to keep yourself fit?'

Ariel looked at the major and asked candidly, 'hey! You aren't going to recruit me into the army, are you, Major?'

'Moshe,' Pesach corrected him. 'As a matter of fact, I was thinking along those lines.'

'The army!'

'Shin Beth. No uniform. No drill. There's a great difference,' came the persuasive answer. 'Would you consider enrolling for a short period?'

Eyeing Pesach levelly and fingering his chin, Cohen asked, 'how short a period?'

'Four weeks at the most.'

'In connection with Project Sonneberg, I suppose?'

'Right.'

'Full time?' Ariel continued. 'I could help you with the plan in my spare time, Major – I mean, Moshe.'

'I'm afraid you must be absent from your business.'

'For four weeks? What am I supposed to tell Sarah?'

'Your wife?' Pesach inclined his head. 'Perhaps a business trip to Amsterdam to buy precious stones?'

'I've never done that before.'

'Well, it's time to start. Diamonds are cheaper in the Netherlands,' Pesach said mildly. 'Could she manage your business for a month, or so?'

'Certainly she could cope with the customers, but not the workshop. Sarah isn't a goldsmith.'

'Naturally you'd receive compensation for any loss of income.'

'It is not a question of compensation, Moshe,' Ariel responded, then continued warily, 'what exactly is my part in your scheme?'

Pesach's one good eye was full of intent. He drew a deep breath. 'To guide our team and Professor Goldman safely through the mine and out into West Germany.'

Ariel's chin dropped. 'Which means that I would have to return to Sonneberg . . .'

'With you in charge, our task would be only half as difficult.'

Cohen drew his handkerchief and wiped his suddenly perspiring forehead.

'What do you say, Ariel?' Pesach urged him.

'I . . . I don't really know what to say.' Ariel managed a half grin. 'When I came to Israel I thought, I hoped, I had put Germany and the Germans behind me for ever. I never dreamed of returning there, Moshe.'

'Yes – too many tragic memories. I can understand your aversion, but Germany has changed a lot.'

'You don't really believe that, do you?' Ariel replied edgily. 'Perhaps in the west – somewhat,' he added, with the face of one making a heavy concession. 'But not in the DDR – as they call it. Have you ever heard of an important Nazi trial in communist Germany? No, because over there, the Nazis have simply switched their colours and insignia.'

'I agree,' Pesach conceded. 'There were no Nazis in the Soviet Zone, only devoted resistance fighters – all eighteen million of them.'

Ariel Cohen looked out of the window. The afternoon sun streamed down on the street. People bustled along, their faces open, uncaring. He could remember different times, when people shuffled along, broken with fear. Up there in the north, it seemed the sun had never shone. He could not recall it now.

'Yes, *Staats Sicherheits*,' Cohen cited in German. 'Before, it was *Geheime Staatspolizei*.' He stared at Pesach entreatingly. 'Moshe, I don't think I could stand the sight of them again without screaming . . . Their stupid initials, their uniforms, their Teuton *ordnung* and arrogance. The very air would suffocate me there. In every smiling, elderly face, I'd see an assassin lurking.'

There was a pause. Major Pesach seemed deep in thought. At length he glanced up and said with gravity, 'I'm not in any way going to force you to return there, Ariel.' His voice was contrite, but then he added suavely, 'think it over and decide later – after a couple of days.'

'That makes it sound rather urgent.'

'It is urgent.'

Cohen nodded his head, smiled ironically and said, 'it is very difficult to refuse, Moshe. When lives depend on my response, or might depend.'

'You accept?' Pesach asked eagerly.

'I owe that much to Israel, don't I?' came the answer. Ariel downed the rest of his beer, discarded the empty tin and looked directly at Pesach. 'You can count me in.'

'I am very glad to know that, Ariel. You are a brave man.'

'Or a bloody idiot.'

'What do you mean?'

'That the communist STASI might finish the job where the Gestapo failed.'

'Come now,' Pesach urged him. 'Don't be so pessimistic.'

'Pessimistic? I'm already fighting my panic.'

'You will be in the company of our best professionals.' Pesach was irrepressible, Cohen thought. The major could exert pressure as easily as he could resist it. 'One of them is a veteran of the Entebbe raid.'

Ariel's grim expression did not change. 'Idi Amin was only a stupid bully surrounded by an army of trash he laughingly called troops. For all their shortcomings, we cannot say the same of the East Germans. They graduated from Soviet schools.'

'True enough. But we too are fairly efficient. You need not fear them.'

'Is there a medicine against fear?'

'Sure. Violence disperses any feelings of inferiority, and also fear.'

'I am not a violent person.'

Pesach smiled benevolently. 'You can leave the violence to my boys. They are professionals.'

Ariel let out an exasperated sigh. '*La'azazel*,' he swore in Hebrew. 'One may only die once.'

Pesach nodded. 'Yes, a philosophical approach helps.'

The conversation reverted to the business of the raid.

'If I understood you, we shall be using a winch to descend into the mine,' Ariel said.

'Which Lieutenant Karlim made use of,' Pesach replied, happy to see Ariel safely on the side of his project now.

'The first level is 75 metres below the surface. That's like going down the side of a fifteen-storey building.'

'The winch, according to Karlim, has foot and handholds and also safety clasps. It's still in pretty good condition.'

'How old is Professor Goldman?'

'Almost sixty.'

'A risky business.'

'There will be a doctor in the team to help the professor. Dr Darit Efrati.'

'A woman!' exclaimed Ariel. He wanted to add that no woman should be involved in such an expedition, but Pesach's upraised hand took the wind out of his protest.

'Darit is a reserve lieutenant in the army, and she volunteered for the mission.'

'Like myself?' Ariel quipped.

But the major continued. 'Goldman suffers from a heart disorder and may need medical attention under stress.'

Ariel Cohen rolled his eyes. 'On top of everything else?'

'I'm certain the professor will manage it. We know he wants to be free, to get out of Russia.'

'Let us hope . . . how are we to get into East Germany? Not on Israeli passports, I presume.'

'Captain Harari and Dr Efrati are going from France, posing as a French couple. Lieutenant Jorv Amran will be a Libyan businessman, and you – a Hungarian tourist.'

'Don't say you have —'

'Certainly. Passports, identity cards, driving licences – hundreds of them,' Pesach interposed. 'And you will enjoy one significant advantage, Ariel. Hungarians have free movement in other communist countries.'

'It must be a damned good Hungarian passport,' Cohen said meditatively.

'It will be good enough to get you anywhere in the world

except, of course, to Hungary. You do speak Hungarian and you know the country, so why worry?'

'I don't know a thing about present-day Hungary.'

'You will take an up-to-date refresher course.'

Ariel thought to himself, Major Pesach has the instant answer to all questions.

4

HAVING HEARD all about Major Pesach's plan in detail, Captain Harari's immediate reaction was an immense sense of pride for being part of a relatively small army detachment which served not only the country, but also Jews in difficulty anywhere in the world, regardless of the dangers. A crack unit whose commanders were capable of planning complex missions and executing them brilliantly.

There had been many daring actions in the past; also postponements, alterations, but never a failure. He felt unreservedly enthusiastic, and when his superior queried his opinion, Harari answered airily that he was already feeling like James Bond, looking forward to meeting the five pretty girls who ought to go with the Sonneberg script.

Major Pesach was amused. 'Five girls, no,' he replied, implying that Shin Beth didn't have the sort of money American film producers had at their disposal. One girl, however, Harari would have. Dr Darit Efrati from Jerusalem, although she was certainly no playgirl. Harari considered this fair enough, under the circumstances, especially when Pesach informed him that Darit was to act the role of Harari's wife during the trip. In theory only, the major added with emphasis, and cautioned Hadar to behave himself with Darit. He did not want to risk a 'divorce' half-way to East Germany. Dr Efrati had set certain preconditions which Harari would have to respect. The young captain laughingly agreed to be a good boy. Pesach suggested that he should go to Jerusalem and meet her.

Jorv Amran, of course, voiced no objections about the coming adventure behind the Iron Curtain. In the past he had posed as an American tourist in Damascus, and then in Latakya – to which town he would derisively refer as the southernmost port of the USSR – so no communist bug-a-boo could ever scare him. On the contrary. He regarded the mission as another challenge, a kind of war game with live ammunition, a real-life thriller.

He said he liked thrillers.

Such as freeing a Russian Jew from behind the Iron Curtain and taking him to Israel. And Goldman was not just any Jew, but a gifted scientist who had been working on missile guidance systems, including the various SAMs now in Syrian hands.

He adored Major Pesach, the *pacha*, as they had nicknamed him long ago, and considered him a genius who should be named Minister of Defence for the good of Israel. Not that the major would willingly accept such a promotion. Pesach seemed perfectly content with his present position. Eichmann, Entebbe, the railroading of a complete Russian radar installation from Egypt proper, now this Sonneberg business – all engineered by Pesach – gave him ample credit. Already he was toying with the idea of sabotaging a nuclear reactor presently under construction near Baghdad. He had dispatched a couple of agents to Iraq, one of them an absolutely trustworthy Arab, and was familiar with Iraqi progress. Jorv Amran was sure that Pesach would know the colour of the socks President Saddam Hussein had been wearing the last time he had inspected the construction site. Shin Beth possessed limited resources and only a handful of picked agents, but they were well placed.

So, Amran's response to Pesach's latest idea was a flat, 'when are we leaving?' although initially he wondered why they couldn't do the job in Romania – closer and also easier. No collapsed mine galleries to clear and play the mole in. There was also the Black Sea, an ideal escape route. Professor Goldman could take a quiet afternoon walk along the shore, or even better, get a rubber dinghy and go fishing. Amran would land a small seaplane nearby and whizz off to Israel without unnecessary delays. He suggested this alternative quite seriously and, knowing his impulsive subordinate, Major Pesach let him carry on for a while before gently reminding Jorv of Romania's unique position with regard to Israel. Certain political subtleties, such as not involving the only communist bloc country maintaining diplomatic ties with Israel in an anti-Soviet kidnapping ploy, would never occur to Amran.

No, Professor Goldman must come through West Germany. The Sonneberg mine was the only way. Accepting this, Jorv settled down with Pesach to learn all the details of the forthcoming mission.

The next day Captain Harari and Lieutenant Amran met again with Major Pesach for a further debriefing.

Amran again began to scan the Sonneberg plans. He paused at the name of Abdul Jafer, a Shin Beth agent in East Berlin. His chin lifted, and he looked at Major Pesach, puzzled.

'Abdul Jafer? Doesn't sound like a kosher name to me.'

Smiling, Pesach handed him a top secret file marked Lt. Adin Karlim, alias Abdul Jafer, alias many other Arab names. 'He has been stationed out of Israel for nearly three years,' the major explained. 'Most of the time he's been in Syria, and then in the Lebanon training PLO guerillas.'

'What for?' Amran asked, baffled.

'Better to fight against Israel,' Pesach replied in a matter-of-fact tone. Now even Harari was astonished. Throughout their years with Shin Beth they had never even heard the name Adin Karlim, let alone met him, although they all served in the same small outfit. They stared at the photo of a young signal corps lieutenant, not more than twenty-five years old. Returning the folder to Pesach, Captain Harari remarked somewhat sourly, 'we are senior members of the grand *mispoche* yet it seems we still have a lot of catching-up to do.'

With a perfectly innocent expression, Major Pesach opened his hands and mysteriously quoted Hamlet. 'To be or not to be, that is the question,' meaning the life-or-death importance of maintaining the absolute secrecy of Karlim's identity. 'You will meet him in East Berlin.'

'How on earth did he manage to get in there?' asked Amran.

'It's a long story, but Karlim is one of our most important agents in enemy territory, and a very successful one too.'

He paused a moment. 'It was Karlim who organised the PLO raid against our radar station at Elon, on the Lebanese border.'

Harari and Amran could only stare.

'But the radar station was demolished!' Jorv exclaimed with incredulous eyes. 'I've seen photos taken after the raid. There were corpses. Everything blasted, including five trucks.'

Major Pesach's one good eye glowed. He seemed amused. 'The radar station at Elon was a mock-up,' he stated, enjoying the situation. 'The corpses were dummies. Naturally they were buried with full military honours to keep the Arab newspapers happy with headlines. The raid was celebrated by them as a great victory; the large-scale Zionist debacle they needed so much.'

Harari turned his head. 'So the action established Karlim's reputation among the Arabs.'

Pesach chuckled. 'And how! The PLO top brass came to congratulate him in person, slapping him on the back in front of the cameras.'

Amran cut in gruffly, 'if I'd been in Karlim's place I would have found a way to blow the bloody *mamzerim* to Kingdom Come.'

'Don't start raving again, Jorv,' Harari warned his friend. Pesach added in a paternal manner, 'to tell you the truth, Jorv, if I had all the present Arab leaders bottled up in a desert wadi, I would leave a way open for them to escape.'

'May I ask why, sir?'

'Can you tell me where else we could get enemy commanders whom we can beat in every battle?'

Harari burst into laughter. Pesach concluded his jest.

'Perhaps their successors would be more capable and give us some real trouble.'

Now Amran too joined in the merriment. How right Pesach was. Keeping a known enemy was preferable to facing an unknown one.

Major Pesach rang his secretary to bring them three beers, and the conversation turned to politics. They skirted the recent five-day Israeli occupation of Southern Lebanon – the 'Blitz' that had netted eight hundred prisoners and over fifty tons of Soviet-made weapons and ammunition – a good business, since Israel would now export them to African and South American clients.

'We are a small nation that for nearly thirty years has been compelled to live in a permanent state of war,' Pesach mused. 'We must conduct our wars economically. Fortunately, we have faithful supporters, including the USSR. For every hundred million dollars-worth of US equipment we also get fifty millions-worth from the Russians – thanks to the Arabs.'

'As long as they're willing to accommodate us free of charge, it's okay for Israel,' Jorv said. 'Moscow is generous. Whenever they send new tanks to Assad, they supply us with the proper shells to destroy them, so Assad will buy more. Fair enough. Business is business.'

They discussed the recent decision of the Knesset to proclaim Jerusalem the Israeli capital for ever. It was a decision which had drawn much local enthusiasm and worldwide disapproval. Amran wanted to wager that the foreign embassies wouldn't be moving from Tel-Aviv. Dismissing this, Harari declined the bet, saying it was only too obvious. Western governments were too busy keeping sweet with the Arabs to consider taking such an action. 'Were the Russians on our side in a reverse situation, they would be first to move into Jerusalem,' Amran said with conviction.

'That's because the Russians don't have to suck up to anybody,' Harari went on. 'When they take over a country they just send in troops, tanks and artillery and swiftly lick the whole place clean.'

'The Russians have long-range policies and execute them ruthlessly, regardless of world opinion, or consequence,' added Major Pesach.

'We should do the same,' Amran prompted. 'Let our enemies and reluctant friends yell their heads off and keep on doing what we consider proper, however undemocratic it may seem.'

'Tell that to the Herut,' Harari suggested.

'Come now – democracy is as dead as a doornail everywhere else,' Jorv argued, again in his element. 'How can democracy survive in a world crowded with powerful and truculent dictators who spit on all the rules? Look at Gaddafi, who by any standards should have been expelled from every international organisation and boycotted into bankruptcy long ago. The same of Khomeini and some of those South American thugs.'

'Gaddafi and Khomeini have millions of barrels of oil to sell to the West every day,' Pesach reminded him.

'They'd have to shove those barrels up in their Goddamn arses, if there were no buyers in the West.'

'The oil cartels and multi-national industries are not the least bit interested in politics, or in humane sentiments,' the major reminded him. 'They're only concerned with making money and would supply hell with fuel if the devil paid in US dollars. They too belong to the "democratic" system and therefore are free to act in their own best interests.'

'That, Major, is why democracy is dead.'

'It seems to be alive and well in Israel,' Harari ventured, but Jorv was not to be stopped.

'Sure it works, but not like it worked in France under General De Gaulle. His parliament had the last word in every matter. De Gaulle ordered "do this", and the assembly replied "yes, sir". With all due respect, Major Pesach, to me not even Menachem Begin is resolute enough.'

'Israel still needs democracy, Jorv,' Pesach commented quietly.

'What Israel needs is another King David, or a Jewish Julius Caesar,' Amran shouted vehemently.

Major Pesach let him rave on.

'Stop being a bloody fool,' said Harari in a disapproving tone.

'I have strong faith in Israel's destiny.'

Pesach cut in. 'We all have . . . over the centuries we have had Ramesses II, the Babylonian exile, the Romans, Masada, the Holy Inquisition, the Russian pogroms and Hitler's genocide tactics. All of them trying to exterminate us. Now Arabs all around us cherish the idea of pushing the Jews into the Mediterranean Sea, but here we are, still around and stronger than ever.'

'But our enemies are around too, sir,' Amran added. 'Only because we were never permitted to destroy them forever. Like that Turkish security officer, Captain Ulutas, said. When another round comes with Syria – as it sure as hell will – we should not stop, but keep going all the way and occupy Damascus. Then we may have peace.'

'Amen,' Harari quipped. 'But, Jorv, you have forgotten about Jordan.'

Missing this taunt entirely in his enthusiastic cascade of suggestions, Jorv only waved a hand dismissing Harari's remark. 'We can leave Jordan and King Hussein to the Boy Scouts!'

'What about the Libyan Adolf?'

'Gaddafi? Let him holler his head off. We don't have a

common frontier. If we did have one, he'd be shouting a lot less.'

He glanced at Major Pesach, who had lit his pipe and was puffing quietly, listening.

'Major, why don't you think up a good plan for knocking him off? You could count me in.'

'Because Shin Beth is neither the Gestapo, nor the KGB, Jorv,' Pesach reminded him.

'Well, in future we should not permit the Arabs, whom we defeat in the battlefield, to win the war in the United Nations – as they always do.' He stopped to look at the major for confirmation. 'Don't you agree, sir?'

Pesach's expression was one of boundless patience.

'To tell you the truth, Jorv, you are most certainly not the chap I would like to see in the Prime Minister's chair. Still, you're a brave soldier and your heart's in the right place.'

Harari broke into laughter and Pesach added for good measure, 'you would probably send our armoured brigades all the way to Baghdad, or even the Yemen. The present Israeli economy couldn't afford such extensive trips, if only because of the cost of Arab fuel.' Jorv didn't find the joke funny at all, so he withdrew fuming into himself Major Pesach steered the conversation back to the planned mission.

'Some of the equipment, including a car which has been dolled-up especially for the occasion, you will pick up in Paris,' he told Harari. 'The rest of the stuff you will need has already been provided by Karlim. He is in constant touch with me.'

'What, from East Berlin?' Harari wondered.

'Why not? East Berlin is not the North Pole, and we do have some friendly embassies there.' Shifting his attention to Amran, he added jokily, 'your Uncle Sam is not involved, though.'

Jorv took the reference to his country of birth in good spirit. 'It doesn't matter. When Professor Goldman vanishes, Uncle Sam's going to take the blame anyway.

According to the communist version of God's truth, all mischiefs that occur behind the Iron Curtain are fostered by the CIA.'

'So much the better,' Harari remarked. 'While the KGB and the STASI are groping in the wrong direction, we'll be smuggling Goldman out to Tel-Aviv.'

Pesach sighed. 'I wish we were already at that point,' he said heavily.

'So, who is this Jacques Moura?' Harari asked, scanning the file in his hands.

'Your contact in Paris.'

'Is he – Yehudi?'

'No. His wife is Jewish, and Moura is an old friend of mine. Also, he knows nothing of your task or your destination.'

The conversation lapsed. Major Pesach rose. 'That's all for the moment, boys.'

'Tomorrow I'll go to see this Darit girl,' Harari announced. 'You said the girl is working in the Haddasah hospital . . .'

'That's right – and she is not "this Darit girl" either, but Doctor Darit Efrati.'

Jorv cut in. 'How about some cuties for me, then?'

Harari turned to him. 'Have you recovered from your spiritual coma already?'

'Get lost.'

'I will – by going to Jerusalem.'

'Can you give me a lift there?'

'Like hell I will.'

Jorv turned to Pesach with a smile. 'And the *gunuf* calls himself a friend!'

'Friend – yes, but not a bedfellow,' Harari reminded him, chuckling.

At this, Major Pesach said sharply, 'I am afraid there'll be no bed waiting for you in Jerusalem, Captain Harari, unless it's for the purpose of sleeping.'

'I was only kidding, as surely you know, Major.'

'I most surely don't . . .'

'Is Doctor Efrati expecting me?'

'Yes. I have already spoken to her about you.'

At the door Harari paused and asked suavely, 'do you happen to have a photo of her?'

'Unfortunately, no,' Major Pesach replied, his brow drawn. 'Darit's file is presently with the General.'

'Too bad,' Amran commented. 'Hadar'll have to buy the cat in the bag.'

'Well then,' Harari bargained. 'Is she pretty?'

'Forget her apparent qualities. Just assume the role of the perfect gentleman and everything's going to be fine.'

'You know, Major Pesach, it's your fatherly heart that I like most.'

Taking their leave the two friends walked out to the parking lot.

It was half past three in the afternoon and as hot as a furnace when Captain Harari manoeuvred his white Jaguar past the town hall in Jerusalem and turned left to skirt the old wall towards the Rockefeller Museum. He crossed the one-time demarcation line with Jordan – that huge exclamation mark behind great-power stupidity, which the Israeli Defence Force had forever erased in the Six Day War.

The great powers, Harari remembered with contempt. How irresponsibly they controlled and decided the destiny of millions of people; naturally other people, not their own. A group of senile politicians and generals somewhere between the age of eighty and the grave would sit down around the table, grab red, blue and yellow pencils, then, puffing cigars and sipping brandy, they would redraw the map of the world at random, disregarding local traditions, human sentiments and economic necessities.

Two Germanies, two Berlins, two Pakistans, two Koreas, two Vietnams . . .

Two Jerusalems.

Separated by coils of barbed wire, limpet-mines, sandbag barriers with gun emplacements and poised bayonets. They had skilfully manipulated Arab hatred and had refused Israel access to that most holy shrine of the Jewish past. Except for David's Tomb near the Zion Gate, Jewish history had been tightly shut behind the ancient walls, from which snipers fired random shots into the Israeli Sector.

However, now once again Jerusalem was united, with free access to every religious shrine for all. Yet not even Israel's closest friends had welcomed the change. It was against Arab interests, and consequently against their own interests – in Arab oil.

Harari stopped the Jaguar and parked at the Damascus Gate to take a short walk and ponder on his recollections of those two turbulent days in June 1967. He had been here then; the troop-carrier had been parked on almost the same spot as his car today. Then, a youthful soldier of nineteen, he had belonged to a platoon of similar young men, none older than twenty-five. They were the trail-blazers, dashing forward along El Wad Street, cutting through wires, climbing over barricades, blasting fences, lobbing grenades and hunting down snipers. Clearing the way to the ancient Jewish Quarters and the Wailing Wall.

They had ploughed through reached the Wall in only forty minutes.

The enemy did not fight, but ran like hares, although they never missed a chance to kill an Israeli when it could be done unpunished. There had been snipers everywhere. Regulars of the Jordanian Army, Al Fatah and civilians, shooting from roofs, windows, balconies – even from the Haram Esh Sharif, one of the most revered Islamic shrines. With foresight, the High Command had spared no effort to minimise Israeli casualties. The front-rank assault troops had been equipped with bullet-proof vests, back-guards and reinforced helmets. The heavy, protective gear had been hell to wear in the heat, but after the combat, Harari had counted four direct hits on his vest, any of which would have been fatal.

Walking down El Wad Street in the peaceful sunlight,

he stopped in front of a narrow archway flanked by two rusted iron rings, with a flight of steps behind. It was here that he had caught a twelve-year-old Arab boy, a member of the Ashbal – the children's militia. The kid had been brandishing a Czech-made Scorpion machine gun in his hand, and was trying to shoot Harari. Fortunately – also for the lad – the magazine was empty and the boy simply did not know how to change it. Harari snatched the weapon from him and thundered, 'what do you want with a gun, you little rat?'

'To kill the Jews with,' the boy replied defiantly. He did not say Zionists, or Israelis, but Jews. The age-old battle cry . . . A familiar echo from past millennia.

Kill the Jews!

Now they could no longer kill Jews without punishment.

Harari grabbed the boy by the collar. He would never forget his face, smeared with dust and gun-grease, large, dark eyes awash with defiance and fear. He slammed him against the wall and tore the gun away from him. All courage now wiped from his face, the young boy paled, wet himself and begun to howl. Harari had fought down his loathing and instead of putting a slug in him, he grabbed a length of plastic hose, dragged him across his knee and gave him the thrashing of his life.

Then he kicked him and sent him back home.

Mustafa, that was his name . . . Perhaps he was in the PLO now, or else already dead. Suddenly, Harari wanted to know what had become of him.

He also recalled those first awestricken moments before the Wailing Wall, hitherto inaccessible to the Israelis. Bullets were still whizzing overhead when the first soldiers to get through had halted to say a brief prayer of thanks for Jehovah's benevolence. But they did not pray alone there for long. Daring the perils came small groups of civilians, young and old, the shabby, drawn-faced but rejoicing survivors of eighteen years of Jordanian rule, to greet the liberators and join them in prayer.

It could have been yesterday, the memories were so

vivid for Harari. But, looking around the busy street filled with cars, vendors, pretty girls bustling along, it might never have happened at all.

Harari returned to his car to find a young policewoman standing by, ready to give him a ticket.

'Is this your car, sir?' she asked with polite authority.

'Unfortunately, yes,' he said, flashing his best smile for her benefit, trying the humorous approach. Sometimes it helped.

Though not in her case.

'I am sorry, but it is prohibited to park here,' she said crisply, ignoring Harari's jest. 'Can I have your registration papers, please?'

Harari fumbled in his wallet and handed the documents over to her, conversing amiably all the while. 'I've been taking a walk along here, trying to recall the past.' He maintained a serene expression and the proper tone while she scrutinised the papers with writing pad and pen at the ready.

She glanced up. 'I see you're a captain in the army.'

'That's right. Captain Hadar Harari – and this is exactly the place where we stormed the Old City back in 1967. I couldn't just drive past without looking,' he added with a smile. 'Patriotic sentiments.'

Her hand holding the pad dropped to her side.

'You were here?'

'In the first assault battalion to storm the Damascus Gate. It was hot too . . . Are you from Jerusalem?'

'Yes, I was born here.'

'You must have been very young at the time.'

She laughed gently. 'I was only young then.' Pad and pen vanished into her shoulder bag.

A Traffic Police car drew up in front of them and a young policeman leaned out of the window. 'Everything all right, Chana?'

She waved a casual hand over her shoulder. 'Shalom.'

The policeman drove off. 'My brother,' she said, then, reverting to her former authoritative stance, she added,

'Captain Harari, the next time you visit Jerusalem, do please pay more attention to traffic signs.'

'I will – and I would also like to pay more attention to Constable Chana.'

She smiled, tossed back her braids and made a sweeping gesture with one hand. 'This is my usual beat. The whole of the Hativat.'

'I'll remember.'

She saluted smartly and he drove off, taking the pictur-esque road up on the Mount of Olives to the Haddasah Hospital where Dr Efrati worked.

The receptionist sent him to Room 22 on the second floor in the modern annexe. The word CYTOLOGY was lettered on the opaque glass door. Harari knocked politely and a woman's voice invited him in.

Darit Efrati was sitting next to a powerful microscope, pouring coffee from a percolator into a plastic cup. She was a young woman, in her mid-twenties, with a perfect oval face, long dark hair and almond eyes. Looking at her, Harari's first reaction was an enthusiastic, 'God bless Pesach.'

Darit was beautiful. She was not wearing engagement or wedding ring, which Harari wondered at. So beautiful a woman in a place probably crowded with handsome colleagues?

'I've come to see Dr Darit Efrati,' he began politely, but turning on his Charming Smile Number One.

'I am she,' came the unceremonious reply. 'And you must be Captain Hadar Harari, my new "husband", as arranged by the Pesach Marriage Agency in Tel-Aviv.'

She is spirited, too, he thought, and decided to answer her in a similar manner. 'And looking at you, Doctor Efrati, I sincerely wish all this was for real.'

It went down well. Darit broke into a short, rippling laugh. 'Thanks for the compliment, Captain . . . Also, you may drop the "doctor" *et cetera*, and call me Darit.' She put out a slender hand in greeting. 'Shalom, and welcome to Jerusalem.'

82

'Shalom, Darit.' He took her hand and held it longer than usual. 'You, Darit, should also drop the "captain" *et cetera*, and call me Hadar.'

'Well then, take a seat, Hadar,' she gestured to a vacant chair. She asked, 'Would you like a cup of coffee?'

'Yes, please,' he accepted the offer without hesitation. Not because he really wanted it, but rather to get Darit out from behind the desk. She rose and walked to a table near the door to fetch another plastic cup. Harari's eyes followed her willowy shape and were satisfied with what they saw. Of medium height with lovely legs and hips. Just the right proportions. Fine style of walking; sexy, but not provocatively so.

Hail Major Pesach and his Project Sonneberg . . . A trip for three weeks with a girl like Darit!

'Milk and sugar?'

'Huh?' He was lost for an instant.

'*Dear* Hadar,' she prompted him.

His gaze lifted. Darit giggled softly. Harari cleared his throat. 'Black – one spoon of sugar . . .'

She filled his cup and offered him the sugar bowl.

'Help yourself.'

She seemed perfectly at ease, so Harari opted for a similar stance. 'Thanks, *dear* wife of mine.'

Darit laughed and they sat sipping coffee, exchanging reminiscences about their respective jobs, about the city. After a brief pause, Darit got back to the business of Project Sonneberg.

'Major Pesach called me yesterday and informed me of your coming.'

'Do you know him personally?'

'Yes. At least, I've met him once. He came to see me last week.'

'And you agreed?'

'To be your wife?'

'That's the one thing, Darit, that I'm really happy about. I mean, that you have agreed to take part in this mission.'

She looked at him with large, innocent eyes. 'Isn't it important for Israel?'

'Very important.'

She drew up her shoulders. 'Then what's so drastic about my posing as your wife? Anyway, I am independent of other ties.'

'Thank God!' Harari commented.

She chuckled. 'Not because of the assignment, I presume?'

'No, it's a big private relief.'

'Tch, tch . . .'

He asked searchingly, 'Did our pacha tell you where we are going, and why?'

'Only vaguely. A very hush-hush mission somewhere in Eastern Europe, lasting a few weeks. I am to look after an elderly Russian Jewish defector who has a slight heart condition – angina – and to help escort him safely to Israel.'

Harari shook his head. 'That was very lightly put, Darit.'

'Why not? Aren't we supposed to be visiting Paris, Zurich, Vienna and all that?'

'Paris, Zurich, Vienna – yes. The "all that" is the problems we might encounter when we get to communist Germany.'

If she was surprised, she didn't show it.

'I've never been to a communist country before.'

'You haven't missed anything.'

'We'll be travelling on French passports?'

'Yes. You do speak French, don't you?'

'*Mais bien sûr* – I graduated in France. Got my diploma at the Sorbonne.'

'I was born in Israel, but my parents were French,' interposed Harari.

'I'm a *sabra* myself,' Darit said. 'My father was British, my mother Polish. They lived in the kibbutzim at Hesho Ha Maala.'

'A nice place,' Harari remarked.

'Yes – now. It wasn't at all nice when the Syrians had their artillery stationed on the Golan Heights.'

Another cup of coffee. Some more silent gazes. Then Harari asked, 'Do you like travelling, Darit?'

'Ah, you mean, do I like travelling in the company of my husband?' Her eyes danced.

'For the sake of our mission, of course,' Harari replied serenely.

'Oh, but of course,' she responded in a mocking tone. 'Only for the sake of country and flag.'

Harari went on reassuringly. 'We can, of course, sleep in separate rooms, at least before entering into Czechoslovakia and East Germany, where such an eccentricity might draw unwanted attention.'

'Of course . . .' The meaning was clear. 'As for the rest of the mission, Major Pesach has reassured me.' She paused before continuing in a near-perfect imitation of the major's voice. 'Captain Harari is a complete gentleman and absolutely reliable. I can vouch for him, Doctor Efrati. He would never take liberties – because of the situation.'

At that she burst into a fit of laughter, while Harari rolled his eyes and said with pretended dismay: 'Oh, dear God,' he said in faintly despairing tones. 'How I adore the pacha's good heart. He really cares for his own, doesn't he?' He leaned over and took Darit's hand. She let him hold it.

Feeling more confident now, Harari said suggestively, 'But it is also the good Major's wish that we should become well acquainted.'

She cast him a level look. 'How well?'

Harari grinned. 'Substantially well.'

'Why do you have to grin so gleefully?'

'This is my most innocent grin,' he protested, all cheer now. 'But I'll try to behave like a good boy.'

'I do hope so.'

'Still, looking at you – it'll be the hardest part of our mission. Worse than playing football with the KGB. Look, you've been my "wife" for only half an hour, but already you are trying to run the household.'

85

She eyed him mischievously, while it occurred to Harari that Darit was fragile, not well prepared for so hard a task. Suddenly he was overwhelmed by a feeling of tenderness towards her. The pacha and his big ideas. How could he ever have coaxed Darit into accepting the job? She was someone to be petted and cared for. Deep within he rejoiced at the thought of having her along, all for himself, but at the same time he dreaded the possibility of her getting hurt – injured, captured, or even worse.

'Hadar, you seem very preoccupied.'

He looked up. Toying with her fingers, folding and unfolding them, he asked with gravity, 'Aren't you at all concerned?'

She smiled understandingly. 'Would it change anything if I were?'

'Darit, this job is going to be dangerous. At least, the latter part of it will be.'

'You mean the trip through the ruined coal mine?'

'You already know about it?'

She nodded. 'Kind of intriguing.'

Harari shook his head in silent disapproval. She must have sensed his genuine concern for her, because she reached out and gave his hand a reassuring squeeze before gently withdrawing it.

'I've been in the army too, Hadar. And not in an elegant hospital somewhere in the rear, but right up at the front. In the Sinai, on the Golan Heights . . . seldom more than half a mile from the fighting. I treated our wounded boys where the medics found them; in foxholes, in wrecked tanks and lorries. Once, I had to amputate a mangled foot on a poor young lad under a burning troop-carrier while shells were still exploding left and right. You need not worry on my account. I have never yet lost my head under stress.'

'If the communists should capture you . . .'

'I'd be jailed. Perhaps for years, but afterwards I'd come home just the same. When I accepted Pesach's offer, I also accepted the risks that go along with it. Had the Arabs captured me on the Golan Heights, it would have been much worse than going to a communist jail.'

'Don't even talk about it, Darit.' Harari grunted, horrified at the idea of Darit in Arab hands.

She added with a lovely smile, 'Anyway, I will have good companions to protect me.'

'You certainly will.'

Then his face darkened for an instant. 'But always remember, we might be killed.'

'*Dulce et decorum est pro patria mori*,' she responded in Latin.

'*Ignoramus et ignorabimus*,' Harari answered in a similar vein. 'But I would prefer to return together with you.'

'And all the others.'

'Of course.'

She suggested that they should continue the discussion at her place, but on seeing Harari's Jaguar, she promptly decided to leave her somewhat battered old Opel Kadett in the hospital parking lot and have a ride in his elegant sports car.

'I've never been in a car like this. It's a British make, isn't it?' she asked, while he opened the door for her.

'Yes. Welcome aboard.'

Darit's appreciative eyes scanned the elegant interior and she breathed a low whistle. 'Does she really go that fast?' she queried, pointing at the speedometer. 'Almost two hundred?'

'Not quite. One hundred and seventy – yes, but that's in miles.'

She belted herself in and he started the engine. 'Which way are we going?'

'Straight on.' She indicated the direction.

Harari circled Mount Scopus, down to highway 30, then raced towards Jericho, watching Darit's long hair streaming out in the wind.

Five miles outside the city he pulled up at the side of

the mountain road that afforded a panoramic view of the town below, surrounded by its Biblical hills.

'How do you like it?'

'Splendid. This car must have cost you a fortune,' Darit said, combing her hair back from her face with her fingers.

'Jaguars don't come cheap,' he agreed. 'Not even in England. And adding on the duties and taxes for Father State . . .' He shrugged and added, 'well, other people have expensive stamp collections, coins, pictures, carpets. My hobby is fast machines. I have an Alfa Romeo, too.'

She chuckled. 'Are you keen on collecting cars?'

'And motorcycles. I have two of them as well.'

'Two?'

'A BMW and an Italian Guzzi.'

'Yours really must be an expensive hobby,' she commented. 'I didn't know the army paid that well. Or do you have your own money?'

Harari smiled complacently. 'The job I do for the army brings in certain premiums, and I have no family to support.'

'So you spend all your money on tax, insurance policies and petrol,' she concluded airily. 'Have you never been married?'

Immediately she saw that she should not have asked. Harari's face darkened. He turned away and gazed towards the shimmering, already crimson skyline. 'Yes, I've been married – for less than one year,' he said heavily. 'PLO terrorists killed my wife in an attack against a crowded supermarket. She was six months' pregnant.'

She reached for his hand and murmured with sympathy. 'I'm so sorry, Hadar. I shouldn't have asked.'

'You couldn't know . . . It happened a long time ago.' He patted her hand. 'Let's go back to town now.'

'May I drive?'

'Be my guest, Darit.'

Slipping sideways, he lifted her over his lap and into the driver's seat. Her hair, silky and soft, brushed against his face; he liked her scent which invaded his nostrils. She studied the gears. He showed her how they worked.

Darit drove back to the city, cruising along the wall and past David's Tomb at the foot of Mount Zion, where she turned into the driveway of a small, whitewashed house in a minute garden set with azaleas and hibiscus beneath two gnarled old lemon trees. 'This is where I live,' she announced cheerfully. 'My house is supposed to be seven hundred years old.'

'Any ghosts?'

'Oh, hundreds! Much midnight creaking and cracking. I'm used to them, though.' She laughed.

Harari followed her over the pebbled path and through an antique, massive door with genuine medieval locks and bolts, into a dark, cool hallway. She opened the shutters to let in the cool evening air, then drew the blinds and curtains and turned on the lights. Harari saw ancient stone walls and a splendid floor, rafters cracked with age, all coloured and lacquered. Around the living room there were tastefully arranged matching old oak chairs, tables and chests, and shelves laden with valuable antiques: pottery of many different periods, bronze and copper utensils, clay figurines, vases and glass jars, some of them expertly reconstructed and secured with restorer's wire. He found more packed shelves in the dining room. A rectangular green billboard displayed swords, arrow and lance-heads, helmets, shields, and a rare chain-mail tabard in fine condition.

Harari whistled softly. 'You have quite a museum here, Darit. My compliments.'

'I love antiques, and I've been collecting them all my life. Most of them I found myself.'

'Oh really? Where?'

'In the Negev – near Avdat.' She gestured over to the shelves. 'This is my hobby, my little obsession. Whenever I get a few days off work at the hospital, I'm to be found out in the middle of nowhere, sifting through sand and digging holes.'

Harari said evenly, 'I have the notion that we are going to do plenty of sifting and digging together.'

'Are you also fond of old things?'

He smiled at her but, instead of answering, he pointed at the billboard. 'The two amphoras over there are mistakenly labelled, Darit. They are not Roman, but much older. More likely Phoenician. The four lance-heads on the extreme left are Egyptian, the rest Assyrian. The helmet is Roman.' He stepped closer and examined the chain-mail tabard. 'I'm not quite sure about this, but it may be a relic from the Crusades. In any case, medieval. Those small, coloured glass jars probably belonged to a Roman lady and contained her scented ointments.'

Seeing her baffled expression, he added by way of explanation, 'I graduated in archaeology at university, and indeed have a small collection of my own.'

She tilted her head and stared at Harari with her hands on her hips and a mischievous look in her eyes. 'Do you know what I think, Hadar?' she began, stressing each word. 'Our mutual benefactor, Major Moshe Pesach, may well have had some far-reaching ideas in his head when he decided to "marry" us.'

Harari grinned. 'Yes, come to think of it. Perhaps there are just a few too many coincidences – common interests – for only a short trip together. Our pacha may well have acted with a certain long-range deliberation.'

'Or possibly he consulted one of his computers.'

'A very clever computer, I should say. At least it made the right selection.' He smiled warmly at her.

'I'm going to tell Pesach to change profession and become a marriage counsellor.'

Harari lowered himself down onto the sofa and tapped the cushion with his palm, beckoning her. She settled next to him. 'Let's see,' he began with pretended thoughtfulness, 'what we have in common so far.'

'Okay, you begin.'

'I am a captain in the army, thirty-two years old and devastatingly handsome,' he began.

'Pooh, pooh – what vanity!'

'All right . . . ruggedly handsome. Anyway, I'm presentable.'

'That sounds a little closer to the truth,' she taunted gently. 'And I am a lieutenant in the stand-by reserves, twenty-seven years old.'

'And smashing,' he cut in. 'Just the right combination. Attractive people are always drawn to each other.'

'Common Interest Number One,' Darit said wryly. 'Now, about this mutual attraction bit. What do you mean?'

'I feel . . . strange vibrations.'

'Don't fall off the sofa, my dear.'

'Well, don't you feel something similar?'

'Butterflies in my gut.'

'You see!'

'Because I haven't eaten anything since lunchtime.'

'Now you've spoilt everything.'

'All right, I'll be good. Go on.'

'We are both university graduates.'

'Point Two.'

'Both interested in archaeology.'

'Common Interest Number Three.'

'We both studied Latin.'

'And also remember some of it. Five.'

'Our adventurous dispositions.'

'Six.'

'Good sense of humour, and we like to tease others.'

'You sound like Pantagruel. Seven.'

'Neither of us is married.'

'Our pacha has thought of everything. Eight.'

He looked her in the eyes and cooed. 'I feel the distinct sensation that we are already falling in love . . . Nine?'

Darit threw back her head and let her tingling laughter rise up in the air.

'Are we?' she teased him.

'You may ask that question again in more personal terms.'

'Are you?'

'Let's say I'm slipping down the slope. What about you?'

'I'm holding on to the ledge for dear life. I've never been in love, and it scares me.'

'Just let yourself go and slide down into the happy abyss. How many points do we have?'

'Eight.'

'We have already counted nine.'

'Oh, no we didn't,' she protested gaily. He wanted to slip an arm around her waist, but she twisted away, laughing, and shook an admonishing finger in front of his nose. 'My – you do like to drive fast. Remember, you're supposed to be the perfect gentleman, very reliable and . . .'

'Don't be a witch.'

'There's a witch in every woman.'

'Then read my mind, O Wicked One.'

She laughed again. 'If I could do that you'd probably be court-martialled.'

'What for?' he asked.

'Carnal violence against a fellow officer.'

He grabbed her by the arms and drew her closer, urgently now. 'Don't tease me, Darit. You're too damned attractive to taunt.' His eyes devoured her inch by inch.

She said quietly, 'Pesach told me that you play chess.'

'Do you?'

'I know how to lose, but I do it tenaciously.'

'We have Mutual Attraction Number Ten.'

'Nine.' She corrected him and rose.

'Why did you get up?' he queried a little sulkily.

'For safety's sake, Captain Harari. Would you like something to eat? A drink, perhaps?'

'Some tea and a sandwich or something, please.'

'I'm hungry myself,' she replied, and began to set a small, round table, then put on the kettle. And she is a doctor of medicine, Harari thought. What a girl. Educated, intelligent, spirited. Mama would have been happy to meet her.

Darit brought to the table some English ham. 'I don't keep kosher,' she announced. 'Do you?'

Harari shook his head. 'I adore ham.'

'And fried eggs?'

'Yes, please.'

A few minutes later she put the light meal on the table and they sat down to eat. Harari said, between bites, 'Darit, I think Pesach is right. We should go under the *chupa* and get married right away.'

'May I ask why?'

He shrugged and answered flatly. 'Well, for one thing, we could pool our antique collections and open a big museum to the public.'

She put down her knife and fork and went into another fit of happy laughter. 'Is that all?'

'Of course, we could also pool some other resources.' He lifted his cup of tea. 'Cheers.'

'Hadar, I get the impression that you have a one-track mind.' She responded in the tones of a strict schoolmistress. 'A genuine one-track mind.'

'It runs in the right direction.'

'So much confidence after only two hours of "marriage".'

Instead of answering he pushed back his chair, walked around the table and lifted her bodily from her chair to kiss her. Her mouth was warm, slightly buttery from their meal. This time she did not recoil.

With sudden passion she returned his kiss and her reluctant arms relaxed and slipped around his neck.

'Mutual Attraction Number Ten?' he whispered into her ear.

'Yes,' she whispered back.

She would not let Harari look for a hotel room that evening. Instead, she set up a comfortable but makeshift bed for him on the living room sofa. Much to his chagrin, she slept in her own room.

5

Landing at Orly Airport just south of Paris, the four of
them, Harari, Amran, Ariel Cohen and Dr Efrati, collected their suitcases and Darit's shoulder bag, hailed a
taxi and went straight to Moura's garage near the Etoile.
It was a moderate basement establishment in the Rue des
Acacias, comprising an office, a store room for spares and
just enough space to accommodate five cars.

When the Israeli team arrived there were only three cars
in the garage: an elegant Bentley, a brand-new Chrysler
and a Lincoln Continental – testimonies to the fact that
not all Frenchmen were bothered by high local gasoline
prices.

Acting on their brief from Major Pesach, the Israelis
sought out Jacques Moura, their local contact. He was a
true Frenchman, charming, talkative and irrepressible;
perhaps thirty years old, dark-haired with inquisitive eyes,
and all smiles.

'Shalom, my friends,' he beamed with youthful exuber-
ance, extending both hands. Looking at Darit he uttered
a softly appreciative 'Oo-la-la' and said that he had not
been informed that the new Miss Israel would also be
coming. He scrutinised her with expert eyes and tremendous, grinning charm. '*Enchanté, mademoiselle.*'

Darit blushed.

Then Moura ushered the visitors into his office, offering
Darit the only chair while he settled the men on a padded
bunk which looked as though at some stage it had been

94

removed from the cab of a long-distance lorry. He sat himself down on a cardboard box full of cans containing engine oil, conversing contentedly. 'So, you have arrived safely. If I had known in advance . . .'

'Monsieur Moura,' Harari began what was intended to be a return of cordiality, but he was promptly silenced by Jacques' raised hand.

'Please, no need for formalities. We are all companions in battle. I'm just Jacques to my friends, including Moshe Pesach.'

This latter revelation somewhat surprised the Israelis. 'Do you know him well?' queried Darit.

Jacques' chin came up. 'Pesach?' he exclaimed. 'He's a grand fellow, *sans pareil* – without equal. Certainly I know him. Whenever he visits Paris he stays at my house in Neuilly. The last time was about two years ago.'

'I remember,' Harari commented. 'He was working on an important case.'

'Working?' Jacques chuckled and winked at Darit. 'I suppose where Major Pesach is concerned one may call it working. I thought he had come to Paris in hot pursuit of sinister enemies of Israel, but all he did when he was here was chase girls all around Montmartre. *Cherchez la femme* – believe me, he was better at it than most of the locals.'

Amran broke into guffaws. 'Did he ask you to round up some good chicks for him, none older than twenty-five?'

'All he asked me to round up was some good quality hotel bills for him to make his expense account more credible once he got back home,' Jacques replied with a grin. 'He needed no help finding women.'

'I can just imagine him,' Darit cut in with merry eyes.

Jacques went out briefly to fetch glasses and a bottle, which he arranged on the small glass-topped table. 'Calvados?' he asked, and began to fill the glasses without waiting for confirmation. Harari, who hardly ever drank, voiced a quiet 'not for me', but got his portion all the same.

'Lion's milk,' Moura declared. '*Santé* – cheers . . . To the success of your mission and the everlasting prosperity of Israel.' They drank to the toast, including Hadar, who thought it impolite not to go along.

'So, tell me. How is life back home?' The little Frenchman bubbled and slapped Harari on the shoulder. 'No more daily shelling from the Lebanon? We followed your five-day house-cleaning session on TV. My wife, Edit, is Jewish, as you probably know. She and her parents are great fans of the Israeli army. Whenever you win a battle they float up into the clouds, propelled by simple enthusiasm.'

The Israelis laughed softly. Amran wanted to say something, but Jacques rattled on like a machine gun. 'And how is the ever-randy Major Pesach? Hasn't he been made a colonel yet?'

'He is still a major,' Harari managed to interpose. 'Now, Jacques, could you show us —'

'He'll be promoted soon enough,' Jacques mused, ignoring the interruption. 'He's a clever man, and by God he gets things done.'

He rose abruptly and excused himself, gesturing towards the garage entrance. 'I have a client,' he winked. 'A very precious one.' He hurried out of the office, a welcoming smile on his face, to welcome an exquisitely dressed elderly lady jangling with gaudy, but extremely expensive jewellery. 'Madame Yvette . . .'

'Is the car ready, Jacques?' she cooed lovingly.

Moura answered with a courteous nod. 'Naturally, Madame Yvette.'

He conducted her over to the white Chrysler and, with a flourish, presented her with a bouquet of splendid red roses that had already been placed on the front seat. 'Roses?' Madame Yvette exclaimed, staring at Jacques. 'Why such a lavish gesture, Monsieur Moura?'

'Why, it's your birthday, Madame,' he replied, smiling politely.

'Oh, how kind of you to remember!'

'Well, Madame, after eight years . . .'

The old lady sighed nostalgically. 'I wish my dear husband could remember it after twenty-eight years together. You really are a darling, Jacques.'

After inspecting the car and declaring that Jacques had done a marvellous job, she drove off and Moura resumed his place in the office with the Israelis again. 'The wife of a filthy rich industrialist,' he explained. 'Electric insulators, submarine cables – six hundred employees. Eight cars in the family to service and no questions asked. The bills go straight to the bank. Quite a few of my clients are like her.'

'The best way to success,' Ariel Cohen commented good-humouredly. Being a businessman himself he recognised Moura's talent for capturing important clients. 'They never bother themselves with the financial arrangements,' Jacques went on. 'They only sign the cheques. Keeping track of payments is the secretary's job. I present my bills and they pay.'

'If you presented the bill for the maintenance of the lunar module they'd pay that too,' Amran cut in with a laugh.

'Probably,' the Frenchman agreed. 'But in exchange for prompt payment I make damn sure that their cars are well serviced, ready on time, and delivered spanking clean. Oh, and I never forget their birthdays!'

Hearing this, Ariel thought, 'By the time we meet again, Monsieur Jacques Moura will be running an establishment with fifty employees.'

A brief pause ensued which Harari used to insert an almost desperate grunt. 'The car —'

'Of course,' Jacques said, scrambling to his feet again. 'How thoughtless of me. Naturally you want to see your car. Come along. Everything is ready.'

He led them to a maintenance bay at the back of the workshop where a shiny black Mercedes limousine was parked on four elevator pads. '*Voilà*,' Jacques exclaimed with pride. 'Here she is.' He opened the hood, the trunk, the doors. 'You'll find the machine has been made up exactly according to Pesach's specifications.'

The team surveyed the vehicle. From the outside it was just like any other Mercedes of its class: sleek, elegant, an expensive car. Except for the jack, spare tyre and snow-chain, the trunk was empty. Harari and Amran walked around it, checking over everything, even lifting the carpets, murmuring between themselves. They examined the roof-lining, the doors, the glove compartment. Harari knitted his brows, rose and asked Moura, 'did Pesach mention, er, certain extras to go with the car?'

Jacques' eyes kindled.

'He certainly did.'

'And?'

'It's all here.'

From his breast pocket he took a sheet of paper, unfolded it, visibly amused by the puzzled look of his visitors. 'The list of extras,' he announced with a wink. Harari and Amran saw only letters and numbers. 'A kind of personal code,' Jacques explained, and began pointing out the cleverly camouflaged equipment, conversing casually all the while.

'One Uzi machine pistol in the engine compartment.' Now that he actually placed his hand on it, the two Israelis could make out the familiar shape, virtually made part of the engine by cleverly applied rubber hoses, wiring and bolts which rendered it unrecognisable. 'The magazines are stashed in the left-hand side of the battery,' their host went on. 'As you can see, both batteries are interconnected and everything's perfectly functional . . . except that the left one contains only two inches of distilled water. The rest is a compartment for spare ammunition – enough room for three hundred rounds. The upper section of the battery is removable.' He demonstrated swiftly how to take it apart. 'Can you see this tubing? It is a double hose. My own invention. The outer one carries hot water, the inner one contains twelve sticks of dynamite. No one's going to check in there. If someone attempts to slacken the bolts they'll get boiling water between the eyes.'

'Jacques, you are a marvel,' Amran complimented the garage owner with enthusiasm. He was very fond of secret gadgets.

'Look here. Filters for gas masks,' Moura intoned triumphantly. He showed them five squat, round cylinders arranged in line on a black steel bar, all connected to the air intakes. There was also a small scuba tank, painted black with a tube seemingly running directly into the carburettor. 'Additional oxygen for high-altitude driving,' Jacques explained. 'No wonder it's such an expensive car. These German engineers think of everything. Of course, it can also be used underwater.'

The Israelis were truly impressed by his ingenuity. But then a vague idea suddenly took definite form in Harari's ever-alert mind, and he asked warily, 'what if we encounter some car-crazy border guard, or a customs officer who might wonder at the unusual layout under the hood?'

'You are right,' Jorv spoke up in support. 'Customs guys are usually familiar with engine layouts. They're trained to suspect anything unusual.'

Moura grinned. 'Naturally we shouldn't leave anything to chance.' From the door pocket he extracted the Mercedes service manual and passed it over to Harari. 'Open it on page four.'

Harari did so and almost keeled over when he saw the double-page colour illustration of the engine compartment with all the individual parts numbered and explained – including the military hardware concealed between them. The illustration was a fake which replaced the original scheme printed by Mercedes, but even the paper was the same.

'Where the hell did you get this printed up?' Harari gasped.

Jacques chuckled. 'You should ask your boss that one. The illustration came from Tel-Aviv, but the rest of the manual is a genuine product of Mercedes Benz, A.G. If anyone gets too curious, push this page under his nose. He won't understand a thing anyway. It's all printed in French.'

'Hail, Pesach!' Jorv interposed and struck his chest in the ancient Roman fashion. 'Do you have any more James Bond gadgets, Jacques?'

'Sure – plenty.'

'Let's see them.'

Moura closed the hood, the trunk and the doors and activated the elevator pads. Smiling mysteriously he invited the Israelis to survey the undercarriage. 'I am not going to tell you anything,' he challenged them. 'Imagine you are customs officers looking for contraband, and tell me what you can find.'

Hadar and Jorv gave the undercarriage a thorough inspection, but neither of them could point out anything suspicious or out of order. Grinning smugly, Jacques deftly unscrewed four small bolts and the petrol tank promptly dropped into his extended hands – or rather, what was a second, outer shell of the proper tank. With Amran to help him, he lowered it to the floor and lifted the metal lid.

'Now look closely.'

Resting on two inches of plain sand and wrapped in strong, transparent plastic sheeting were a pair of automatic pistols, ten hand grenades, five face-masks, a miniature blowtorch outfit and four slim, finned projectiles which Hadar and Amran recognised instantly. 'Yes, bazooka shells,' Jacques announced coolly. 'Pesach thought they might come in handy. Will you help me get it back into place again?'

He replaced the container and tightened the bolts. Amran banged on the petrol tank, which sounded convincingly full. The sand, of course. He stared at Moura. 'Where is the bazooka?'

'Look for it.'

Knowing exactly what to look for, the two men tested the drive-shaft and the twin exhaust outlets, but saw nothing except bona-fide mechanism. 'Check the exhaust system again,' Jacques helped them.

The dual system seemed perfectly regular. The long exhaust pipes swept down from the engine manifold on either side of the undercarriage. Jacques unbolted a straight section of the left-hand outlet, which smoothly detached itself from between the manifold and the principal muffler. From the inside he drew out an inner tube which he temporarily replaced, re-establishing the exhaust outlet. He handed the five-foot outer tube to Hadar.

'Your bazooka.'

'Well, I'll be damned,' was Jorv's only comment.

Jacques laughed. 'What are you up to? Planning to kidnap Brezhnev?'

'No, but something almost as difficult,' Harari replied.

Moura held up a hand. 'Tell me nothing. I don't hear. I don't see. I don't talk.'

'What *are* you doing, then?' Darit interposed for the first time.

Jacques turned to her and said with immense dignity, 'Mademoiselle, I am peeling bills from Moshe Pesach's bankroll, though he is a miserably excellent bargainer who fights over every penny and a real *tête-de-merde* when it comes to paying up.'

Harari rocked on his heels with laughter. Cohen smiled. When the general merriment ceased, Jacques asked, 'did you book into a hotel?'

'Not yet,' said Jorv.

'Fine. I will take you to a small, comfortable one in Neuilly, close to my place. I would put you up myself, but we only have three rooms.'

'Any hotel will do, so long as it's quiet and fairly out of the way,' said Harari.

'Of course, you must come to dine with us.'

'With pleasure.'

Back in the office, Jacques gave Hadar a small leather case. 'Here's the rest of the documentation you're going to need – car papers, insurance, Green Card, passports, driving licences, credit cards issued to a certain Monsieur Pierre Bouvier, commercial director of Usines Dufresne & Cie of Bourg Madam – a southern suburb outside Paris. They make transformers, dynamos, all that sort of stuff. Your Paris address is real, likewise your job. Any chance enquiry regarding your identity would be answered affirmatively.'

'You seem to have thought of everything.'

'Not me. Pesach!' Jacques corrected him. 'He is the procurer. I am only the delivery man.'

'With a magnificent talent for building cars to the owner's specifications,' Jorv retorted.

The Frenchman shrugged. 'My hobby,' he replied and then went on to explain. 'Some years ago, I used to do a little smuggling between Switzerland and France. With the profit from that I opened my garage.'

'And they say crime doesn't pay,' Darit reflected.

Harari chuckled. 'Well, if you commit it for some honest purpose, as Jacques did, it might.'

Jacques took over with pretended indignation. 'What do you mean by saying crime? All I did was recover some of the dough the good Father State had taken off me in income tax, road tax, circulation tax, petrol tax, value-added tax, breathing and shitting tax during the last ten years.'

He suggested that the team should go sightseeing and shopping. Harari had planned to do that anyway. Their Israel-made clothes and shoes would have to be changed for French ones, since nothing marked 'Made in Israel' was to go behind the Iron Curtain.

Moura recommended that they try the Printemps department store on the Boulevard des Italiens, near the Opera House.

'Return here before seven. In the meantime, I'll arrange for your accommodation. Edit will prepare dinner. She really is very keen to meet you.'

At this point Darit drew him aside and the two began whispering between themselves, puzzling Harari. Jacques grinned constantly, and performed a series of quick nods

102

of agreement. '*Très bien*,' he concluded, still grinning. 'No problem.'

Harari stared at them blankly. 'What's the big secret?' he queried. 'You're making me jealous.'

'It is my Parisian charm,' Jacques replied, winking at Darit. 'Go and try out your Mercedes.'

'I hope we aren't going to blow up somewhere around Place Vendôme,' Harari commented, and the Frenchman reassured him.

'Don't worry. You are well insured.'

Darit slipped behind the steering wheel. 'Let me drive.'

'Do you dare to take on our infamous Paris traffic?' Moura asked a little dubiously.

'I lived here for a while. During that time I learned to drive exactly as you locals do.'

'How do the locals drive?' Jacques wanted to know.

'Why, they close their eyes, recite the Lord's Prayer, and give gas.'

'My dear, that's so true!'

There was more laughter, which Hadar did not mind. They needed all the cheer they could get, because there wasn't to be much once they got to East Germany.

He was about to sit next to Darit when Jorv blocked his way, threw open the rear door and beckoned him to enter.

'Would you care to settle your *toches* in the back seat like a playboy – First Class – while I sit next to Darit for a change?'

'Like a good gorilla,' Harari added, and took the rear seat next to Ariel. Darit started the engine and Jacques waved a hand.

'See you later, *mes amis*.'

Amran called from the window, 'say, Jacques – haven't you got any more built-in tricks, such as a passenger ejector seat, for instance?'

Checking the papers he had collected from Moura, Harari's expert eyes quickly noticed that his Green Card had not been validated for travelling in communist countries and paid a mental compliment to Major Pesach. No detail, however small, had escaped his attention. The validation would have disclosed their destination.

He could get the necessary authorisation in Zurich, or Vienna, or in Germany.

Besides, Pesach may even have 'erred' deliberately. It was a habit of his to leave just one or two tiny snags in an otherwise perfect blueprint for his subordinates to discover and correct – a good way to train sharp-minded intelligence operators who, when their lives depended on precision and attention to detail, would search for and discover the mistakes.

He checked all the other documents minutely, looking for discrepancies, contradictions, all of which communist secret police were excellent in detecting.

He found no mistakes. Satisfied, he took his notebook and jotted down: Extend Green Card.

It was seven o'clock in the evening by the time they had finished purchasing their new clothes and shoes. Meeting up once again with Jacques Moura back at the garage, they were then taken to the Chapeau Rouge, a small hotel in Neuilly-sur-Seine, in the centre of a fine park, where accommodation had been arranged, including a separate room for Darit. Harari, who had been entertaining vivid fantasies ever since they left Tel-Aviv, seemed rather rebuffed by this unexpected development, but acquiesced with a resigned, 'our dear Jacques is a king-size *gunuf*.' The Yiddish word for malefactor.

Defending Moura, Darit airily confessed that the idea had been hers.

'Oh, so that's what you were whispering about together in the garage earlier on,' Harari remembered. 'I should have known.'

Whereupon Darit tacitly reminded him of his own disclosure in Jerusalem. 'Did you not say that we could sleep in separate rooms before entering Czechoslovakia?'

'You have a wonderfully retentive mind,' Harari grumbled in reply.

The following two days were spent mostly preparing for the forthcoming mission. Darit purchased a light medical kit and with the help of the embassy physician she obtained those drugs she knew might be necessary for Professor Goldman, and which could not be brought along on account of their Israeli labels.

Having obtained visas, they drove to Switzerland, then on to Austria, leaving some time for sightseeing. Professor Goldman was due to leave Moscow for Bucharest the next morning. Basel, Berne, Zurich, Vaduz in Lichtenstein, Salzburg – where they visited the famous castle – then the Autobahn to Vienna with a short detour near Linz.

Ariel said he wanted to make a brief pilgrimage to the former Nazi concentration camp at Mauthausen, where both his father and brother had perished. Harari did not think that it would be good for Ariel's morale before the crucial part of their mission, but he could not very well object to such a request. He consented with mixed feelings.

6

ARIEL COHEN stood for a while in front of the tall, forbidding grey wall; his companions remained a few paces behind in silence, permitting Ariel to gather his sad memories. They could see that he was fighting back his sobs. After a while, Harari sighed deeply, joined him and muttered, as though to himself, 'if these stones could talk . . .'

Cohen turned slowly. His eyes were filled with tears. He dabbed at them with a paper tissue and spoke in a tight voice that was laden with emotion. 'If these stones could talk, Hadar, they would be screaming. Howling a long, endless cry of agony.'

They walked closer to the massive double-winged gate hung with two high, arched doors. Darit thought that Ariel suddenly looked very shrunken and tired. The entrance was flanked by elevated platforms reminiscent of medieval battlements, each topped with a glass-walled guardhouse, offering an all-round view. The one on the right had had a great marble slab fixed on to it, commemorating the number and nationality of all the prisoners killed in the KZ Mauthausen; gassed, hanged, shot out of hand, in mid-winter doused with icy water until they froze to death, beaten, or simply worked to death; Jews and Christians from every part of Europe. Gypsies. Russian prisoners of war.

To the three young Israelis the camp was only a reminder of recent history. One of many similar tragic monuments to Jewish suffering. They knew of the Holocaust from their

106

elders, from their student years, from books, documentary films, and the Holocaust Museum in Tel-Aviv. But now, the act of physically visiting one of the sites and seeing the hideous relics of that agony, made everything appear different. The hitherto impersonal impressions suddenly became intimate and involving.

Mauthausen, Buchenwald, Belsen, Dachau, Ravensbrück, Sachsenhausen . . .

Auschwitz-Birkenau . . .

Twentieth-century analogues of the Holy Inquisition of Spain, only infinitely more cruel, merciless and deadly.

'Jews from France, Belgium, Holland, Poland, Yugoslavia, Romania, Hungary —' Ariel Cohen recited from long-remembered texts.

'You were born in Hungary, weren't you, Ariel?' Jorv Amran spoke up to distract his companion from his reverie for a short while.

Ariel's face lit with a faint smile and he nodded. 'My ancestors had lived there for centuries. So had the forefathers of many Jews slaughtered here. We contributed to the arts and sciences, to industry and commerce; bled for the country in every war, yet we were never permitted to call it our own. We have always been treated like strangers. Vagrants, belonging to no nation.'

'Now we do have a country,' Darit interposed softly.

'Yes, for the first time since Darius the Great,' Cohen replied with mild irony. 'And it's about time.'

Harari asked, 'How many Jews were living in Hungary before the war?'

'About six hundred thousand – but only some fifty thousand survived deportation in the Budapest ghetto, which the Nazis could not raze on account of the rapid Russian advance. Home-coming rural Jews, who found all their property devastated, settled in the capital. Then their anti-Semite neighbours complained, "We have more *biboldos* than Hitler ever deported."'

The word is a derogatory Fascist term for Jew.

The former SS barracks had been demolished by the

Americans immediately after the war. On their sites now stood a cluster of monuments, erected by the governments of the victimised nations. Only the former Kommandant's office and attached officers' quarters still stood, with its spacious first-floor terrace overlooking the walled reception yard where the new arrivals had been stripped of their belongings and assigned to their respective barracks. Fifteen long barracks, each crammed with prisoners in three-storey bunks. Ten more in the Russian POW compound.

Ariel broke the silence. 'Over there, under the tower by the steel gate, I sat with my father and brother.' His companions said nothing. Casual words of commiseration would have been out of place.

'Do you really want to go inside?' Jorv asked quietly. Cohen shifted his gaze towards him and shook his head. 'No, Jorv. I would prefer not to go inside.'

Instead he guided his companions along a narrow dirt road that ended at a long flight of roughly-hewn stone steps leading to a stone quarry half-way down the hill. 'The Staircase of Death,' Ariel commented quietly, as he walked to an overhang at the top of a hundred-foot-high cliff. This was the spot where his father and brother had been kicked down into the void by SS guards in October 1944.

'"*Fallschirmjaegers*," the guards used to call the unfortunate ones whom they kicked into the abyss, in most cases without any particular reason – only for their own entertainment, laughing about it afterwards, "*Noch ein dreckiger Schmaus weniger.*" One dirty Jew less.'

Later, when they were all slowly walking back to the visitors' car park, Ariel said ironically, 'how strange. For a long time I vowed that I never wanted to see another German face again. Yet here I am, returning, perhaps, to encounter my one-time tormentors, the assassins of my family, my friends. Because the Jew-haters will always be around. They substituted the Swastika with the hammer and sickle, but not their traditions, their convictions. I am still far away from East Germany, but I can already smell the lingering stench of anti-Semitism. I know I am a fool to go back there and give them a chance to kill one more Jew. The only thing that makes this mission worthwhile is that it may help to save a fellow Jew who is much more important than myself.'

Harari put his arm around Cohen's shoulders and said with gentle reproval, 'you shouldn't talk like this, Ariel. We don't have important or unimportant Jews in Israel – only Jews, citizens. And the Germans aren't going to kill you, either.'

'Nevertheless, I feel a strange sense of doom about it, Hadar.'

'Perhaps it would have been better if you had not come to Mauthausen.'

All of them felt a little depressed as the day of separation approached. From Vienna, Harari and Darit were to proceed by car. Jorv, travelling on a Libyan passport, and Ariel, posing as a Hungarian tourist, were to continue by train.

The four were to meet a few days later in East Berlin.

Just before they left, Captain Harari paid a brief visit to a Romanian Jew living in Vienna who was in Major Pesach's employ. He translated the recent Bucharest dailies. A couple of paragraphs informed them of the movements of Professor Jakov Abramovich Goldman, who was presently giving guest lectures in the Romanian capital. Harari even saw a news photo showing the professor in the company of a happily smiling Igor Malcev. He won't be smiling in ten days time, Harari inwardly commented, and noted with satisfaction that – so far at least – everything was proceeding as smoothly as a Swiss clock.

7

ARIEL COHEN and Jorv Amran travelled separately to Prague, arriving safely without incident, and there boarded the same train bound for Berlin via Dresden. Although they occupied the same compartment, they pretended not to know each other; each sat quietly, either reading – or not reading – newspapers appropriate to their disguise, or staring out of the window at the bare spring farmland of Eastern Europe.

At Decin the East German border police boarded the train to check everyone's passports as they crossed the frontier. Having already crossed one communist border, Cohen felt quite at ease in his role. He was calm and unconcerned, and not even the sight of the disdainful German uniforms could dent his confidence. The East Germans looked exactly like Ariel's wartime guards, only their uniforms were without SS lapels and deathshead insignias. Also, they were friendly and courteous.

'*Aus Ungarn* – from Hungary?' asked the overweight sergeant who was in charge. Giving Cohen's passport only a casual glance, he promptly stamped it. 'Ah, yes, the Balaton and the Hortobagy,' he recited the names of the famous lake and plain, to which the accompanying customs officer added good-humouredly, 'yes, and Pick salami, Barack palinka, Tokay wine,' referring to those Hungarian exports beloved all over the rest of Europe, among them apricot brandy. Smiling jovially, Ariel shook his head. He did not have anything to declare and promptly volunteered

110

to open his suitcase. The customs officer laughingly declined his offer. '*Alles in ordung*,' he said magnanimously. 'It's all right. Hungarians in the DDR always come to buy; they're rarely here to sell anything.'

Moments later the sergeant and his companion were busy praising Gaddafi to a politely grinning Jorv Amran. Everything was going according to plan.

'How long will you stay in the DDR?' the customs officer asked Jorv.

'Five or six days, perhaps a little longer. It depends on how well my business goes,' Jorv answered pleasantly.

'What's your line of work, buying or selling?' the sergeant wanted to know.

'Both,' he responded. 'I sell dates and crude oil, buy farm machines and lorries.'

'Have a good time in our country. Hope you do some good business.'

'Thank you. I'll really give it a try.'

Fifteen minutes later the train rolled away from the border and thundered on towards Dresden. When they arrived at the vast main station, Cohen changed to the local train service for Karl Marx Stadt, where his saviour from the concentration camp, Martin Drexler, now lived. Apart from needing some important last-minute information regarding the frontier zone around Sonneberg, he wanted to pay homage to the old engineer, who had been one of the few Nazis to behave humanely in a vast sea of inhumanity during the war.

Jorv Amran remained on the international express as far as Berlin. The two men had planned to meet up again later in the Hotel Grunewald, near Alexanderplatz. Harari and Darit were to book into another hotel. It had been agreed earlier that the members of the team would meet only in public places: art galleries, museums and such like, but never talk of their mission unnecessarily. Not even in the privacy of their hotel rooms.

It was almost five in the afternoon when Cohen arrived in Karl Marx Stadt, formerly named Chemnitz. The train he wanted to catch for Berlin was scheduled to leave at 7.58 p.m. Wasting no time, he took a cab and gave the driver the address. He was driven to a handsome mansion in a hilly suburb, an area obviously inhabited by the communist élite.

He rang the bell and immediately the garden gate snapped open. Cohen walked up to the imposing entrance and was greeted by a well-dressed woman who looked about forty years old. She was handsome, with long, richly blonde braids coiled about the back of her head. He introduced himself to her, giving his name, and stated the reason for his call. He was from Hungary and wanted to pay a visit to Martin Drexler, his wartime acquaintance.

'I am Helga Drexler, Martin Drexler's daughter-in-law. I am married to his son, Herbert,' she replied, offering her hand to Ariel.

He was ushered into a lavishly furnished sitting room.

'Please take a seat,' she gestured over to an armchair. 'I'll tell Martin you're here. He is paralysed these days, you know.'

Cohen pretended not to know. He gasped with surprise. 'I am so sorry to hear that.'

'Does Martin know you?' she ventured politely, but still obviously a little wary of him.

'I don't think he will remember me after all this time. We were together back in '45, shortly before the end of the war.'

'He was in the army then . . . Were you comrades?'

'Not quite,' Ariel shook his head, contemplating whether or not he should tell the truth, then added resolutely, 'you see, Frau Drexler, I was one of the Jewish deportees whom Herr Drexler helped to survive in Sonneberg.'

'Ah, so,' Helga Drexler commented, barely concealing her disappointment – or dismay. 'Yes, Martin always was such an idealist.'

That was crudely put, Ariel thought. As if one had to

be labelled an idealist for saving innocent lives. But the word *Jude* would never bring cheer to German faces. The majority of them, Ariel was convinced, hated Jews; or, at best, despised them. Some were indifferent. A small minority may have felt a kind of remorse. He thought the number of Germans who felt any true affection for Jews could be counted on ten fingers.

A few minutes later Helga Drexler returned and showed Cohen into Martin Drexler's study. As he walked through the door, he saw a young lad of about fourteen come bouncing down the upper-floor staircase. 'Our son, Kurt,' she introduced him casually. He nodded and then turned round to enter the room.

Ariel instantly recognised Martin Drexler, despite his advanced age and frail form. The same high forehead, deep-set blue eyes, strong nose and prim mouth. The old engineer was sitting in his wheelchair behind a large oak desk laden with papers in orderly stacks.

Drexler studied his face for a while, but Cohen could see that there was no recognition in his eyes. Cohen thought this quite natural. There had been so many prisoners in Sonneberg. He put out his hand in greeting.

Soon their mutual reminiscences warmed the formal atmosphere, and if Drexler could not recall Ariel personally, he certainly remembered particular events his visitor cited. After a while, the names of Major Pesach and Simon Wiesenthal popped up, and Ariel then confessed the nature of his visit. With a visibly troubled expression the old man hushed him.

'Lower your voice, please. My daughter-in-law is an active SED member, and my grandson, Kurt, passionately believes in the teachings of Marx and Lenin rather than in God. If you were to ask him who he thinks are his father and mother, he would probably say the Communist Party and the DDR. If that were really the case he would be better off an orphan.'

A knock on the door interrupted their exchange. It opened slightly and Frau Drexler peered in. 'Would you like some tea or coffee, Vater?' she asked, then after a pause a moment too long for good manners, added, 'and you?'

'Tea,' the old man said, and Cohen requested the same. She left, and a moment later Herbert Drexler entered, a lanky, bony man in his early forties who bore a striking resemblance to his father. 'My son, Herbert,' the old engineer introduced him, and added reassuringly, 'we may speak freely in front of him. Thank God his brain hasn't been washed yet.'

'Herr Cohen, you are from Israel?' Herbert Drexler queried aloud.

'Shh, not so loud,' his father cautioned him. 'Herr Cohen is travelling on a Hungarian passport, something our enthusiastic party workers in the family must not find out about.' This was obviously aimed at Herbert's wife and son, but the younger man took it with a wry smile.

'We live in difficult times, and in a different system,' he told Cohen gloomily. 'A system spawned in Russia, where it does not work either. What's more, it's never going to work, because ever since human communities came into existence, man's driving force has been to gain and prosper. Improve his lot, whether with money or power, neither of which can be possessed in the DDR, except, of course, by the party élite.' Then, changing the subject as abruptly as he had embarked on it, he asked Ariel how they could be of help.

Since Martin Drexler was known to and trusted by Major Pesach, Ariel told him the gist of his reason for coming. Leaving out most of the specific details, he explained that there was a possibility that he and his team might use the mine as an escape route. But of Professor Goldman he said nothing.

'Your hunting lodge is situated only half a mile from the frontier zone at Sonneberg. From there we could observe the position and frequency of the patrols.'

The Drexlers stared at him blankly. 'From what you've said, which, may I say, isn't much, your plan sounds like sheer madness,' Herbert exclaimed. 'That mine is impenetrable now. They sealed it up years ago.'

The elder Drexler held up a hand. 'That may not absolutely be so,' he interposed. 'If they have enough time to break down the barricades of rubble, they could possibly get through and reach the West German side. Somehow the Israelis have managed to get hold of a ground plan.' He shifted his gaze over to Cohen. 'Of course you may use the *Jagdhaus*. Herbert will give you the key.'

'We don't want the key,' Ariel said. 'We would rather break down the door. That way, if anything goes wrong, you'd be safely out of the picture.'

Frau Drexler's return interrupted the conversation. They immediately turned to discussing niceties about Budapest, the good wines of Hungary and memories of pleasant vacations at Lake Balaton. While they were talking, it occurred to Ariel how awful it must be when members of the same family could not confide in one another. But, having served the tea, Helga Drexler withdrew discreetly and the talk reverted to its original theme.

Herbert Drexler seemed to be fairly well informed on the latest schedules of the different border patrols. 'I spend most of my weekends at the hunting lodge,' he explained. Then, taking a sheet of paper, he drew a rough plan of the woods around Sonneberg, marking the various approaches to the mine, the positions of sentries, and the regular beat of the border guard. This information, Ariel knew, was what Harari needed the most.

Cohen was invited to stay for dinner, which he politely declined. He wanted to reach Berlin tonight, so after bidding an amicable farewell to Martin Drexler, Herbert drove him back to the railway station in time for the eight o'clock train.

On the day when they were to meet Pesach's East German agent, Lieutenant Adin Karlim, in the Wuhlheide park just outside the city, Harari decided to leave the Mercedes in the hotel car park. He did not want to attract any unnecessary attention to the large luxury car with its French registration plates. To make absolutely sure that no one was tailing them, he first took Darit out on a sightseeing tour down the Friedrichstrasse, stopping frequently to look in shop windows and lingering at the photo display of the Distel cabaret, where he bought two tickets for the evening show that night. Taking the Leipzigstrasse, the two returned to the Unter den Linden, passing in front of the Academy of Sciences where Professor Goldman was scheduled to attend a series of meetings with his East German colleagues.

'Our scene of action Number One,' Harari commented quietly, while Darit took snapshots of the impressive building from which Goldman was to make a leap to freedom. It was Karlim's job to make the initial contact and work out the best route for the professor to leave the city.

Behaving like ordinary tourists, holding hands and chatting merrily, they walked past St Hedvig's Cathedral and the Opera House, then paused briefly to join a crowd watching the ceremonial changing of the guard at the *Neue Wache* – the monument to Fascism.

The guard was comprised of hand-picked young soldiers, the same well-built young men upon whom the communist system bestowed the best traditions of the Nazi Wehrmacht: the strikingly similar uniform, the highly polished boots and the stiff goose-step style of marching. The ceremony was impressive, but Harari was no longer at all surprised that Ariel Cohen should feel depressed in the martial German atmosphere which, here in the DDR, was tenfold more pronounced than in the West. Indeed the same troops could have paraded down the Unter den Linden under the Hitler standards with eagles and Swastikas, and no one would have noticed the difference.

Darit wanted to visit the nearby Museum of German History. But, after strolling through a couple of rooms, she lost interest. The exhibitions were too overtly Marxist in their presentation. Even eighteenth-century events were

116

depicted from this rigid angle, not to mention the section devoted entirely to the early prophets of communism and their latter disciples.

The museum also housed a lavish Islamic exhibition, but almost nothing was shown of German Jewish history, of the holocaust. The few pictures of Himmler's extermination camps and the captions beneath them spoke of the heroism of European resistance fighters with the communists in the first line, tormented by the Gestapo and the massacres of Russian prisoners of war. Obviously, from the East German point of view, the Jews and Israel did not exist.

'Such a shameless distortion of history,' Darit commented on the way out.

'You need not wonder,' Harari replied scornfully. 'According to the communist version of history, it was the Russians who invented everything from the electric light bulb through to the wireless and aeroplanes. Except, of course, the unfortunate inventors didn't get any attention in Tsarist Russia, so the discoveries ended up abroad; were stolen, copied and turned into profit by the mean Western capitalists. That's what they tell their children in school. I shouldn't wonder if they discover one day that Shakespeare was a Russian emigré, despite the fact that his English translations are truly perfect!'

Darit laughed aloud and a couple of people turned to look at her. She played down her amusement and took Hadar by the hand. 'I'm sorry, but it sounded so funny.'

Having crossed the Spree bridge, Harari suggested they stop for a quick snack and coffee, after which they boarded the S-Bahn for Wuhlheide.

Adin Karlim was already there, sitting in his parked Wartburg. He was a lean, moustached, curly-haired man, distinctly Semitic, but possibly more Arab than Jewish. He had obviously recognised Hadar and Darit the moment they left the station, because he left the car and began walking towards the pioneer park, taking a signposted promenade leading into the woods, holding a frisky young Alsatian on the leash. Since Karlim neither signalled nor waited for them, Harari quickly realised that Major Pesach's top agent in East Germany did not wish to be contacted before they were deep in the forest and out of sight of prying eyes.

The venue for their encounter had been chosen expertly. Any casual follower would have been detected immediately, and then they could have cancelled the meeting without making a fuss. The thick canopy of trees and bushes ruled out observation from a distance.

Holding hands, Hadar and Darit strolled after Karlim, looking just like any other young couple out on a casual walk.

Karlim continued to walk alone with his dog for a good two hundred yards before he halted and sat down on a bench facing an elegant white marble fountain. Hadar and Darit sat down next to him.

'*Shalom*, Adin,' Harari greeted his colleague without offering his hand – another rule.

'I'm glad you got here safely, but no Hebrew please, not even between ourselves. I forget my Hebrew while I'm here in Berlin. I must live, think and talk like an Arab. That avoids any slip of the tongue, even when I'm asleep. I have a Syrian room-mate.'

'You are right,' Harari agreed, switching to Arabic.

Then Karlim asked, 'what about Jorv Amran and Ariel Cohen?'

'They are staying in another hotel.'

'And the extra material you were supposed to acquire in Paris?'

'Everything's here.'

'I left some equipment for you in the mine. Overalls and boots. Some other stuff.'

'Any news from our man in Bucharest?'

'Yes, I have received a message. Professor Goldman is leaving Romania tomorrow, for Prague.'

'When do you expect him to arrive in Berlin?'

'Next Monday.'

There was a pause. 'Any idea which hotel he's booked into?' Harari asked.

'In a government guest house in Pankow, heavily guarded by the STASI. Totally inaccessible. However he will be given an official reception at the airport and several meetings at the Academy. A little sightseeing around Berlin has also been scheduled for him. On one of those journeys, I'll make contact with him.'

Harari's brows furled. 'He has an escort, you know.'

'KGB Captain Igor Malcev,' Adin nodded. 'A notorious *meshugeneh*.'

Captain Harari did not agree. 'The KGB is not likely to employ dimwits,' he answered seriously.

Karlim grinned. 'Unless they happen to have well-placed relatives, as has Malcev. Some uncle of his is a high-up in the Supreme Soviet Assembly.'

'In any case, Malcev has been trained to behave like a leech. The professor must find a way to shake him off at the right moment. Long enough to enable him to vanish from sight.'

'In Bucharest he was wised-up by Yehudit, and knows what to do on Liberation Day. Goldman will have an upset stomach and will develop a frequent need to visit the men's room.'

'Until Malcev grows weary of following him,' Harari added.

'Besides, even KGB officers must go to the lavatory sometimes.' Karlim unleashed the Alsatian and threw a stick for him to chase. The conversation reverted to the coal mine. 'Apart from overalls and boots, I've left hardware which might come in useful. It's all on the first-level landing. Eight grenades, another machine gun, picks, helmets, ammo . . .'

'How ever did you manage to get hold of weapons in a communist country, with all the formalities and controls they exercise?'

'Didn't you know? I work for the PLO. I supervise their arms shipments,' Karlim said equably.

'Oh, yes – the pacha told me. What about moving around in the frontier zone, Adin?'

'I got a pass issued to me from the PLO liaison officer in Lichtenberg, but I have an even better idea for your team.'

'Where is Lichtenberg?' Darit cut in.

'A district of East Berlin where the Ministry of State Security is located.'

She said thoughtfully, 'was it not risky for you to tie yourself to the Sonneberg area, Adin? I mean, sooner or later the police are going to discover our escape route. They might put two and two together, especially when they learn about your former presence in the same area.'

Karlin shook his head and replied mildly. 'Thank you for your concern, Darit, but you need not worry. My movements in East Germany are wholly legitimate and invariably are approved by Dr Abd el Bekr.'

'You really have managed to push yourself high up the ladder, Adin,' Harari whistled softly.

'It is necessary to have good connections here.'

'Why? Who is this Doctor Bekr?' Darit queried.

'For all practical purposes, he is Arafat's ambassador to East Germany,' Harari answered.

Karlim added, 'One of Arafat's brothers will be over here too, at the same time as Professor Goldman – probably staying in the same hotel.'

'I presume the pacha is quite happy to have you so well placed here.'

'Why shouldn't he be?' Karlim chuckled. 'He gets a copy of the invoice for virtually every arms shipment destined for Syria.' He opened his arms and rolled his eyes. 'Many are the ways of Allah, but most of them lead to Tel-Aviv,' he intoned.

Laughing quietly, he rose. They strolled deeper into the woods and talked about the mine. Now Harari wished he had brought Ariel Cohen along. Karlim suggested a second encounter. 'The day after tomorrow. At the same time.' And he told Harari that a small team of Israelis would be

120

waiting for them on the West German side under the command of Major Yoel Shanan of Mossad. His announcement surprised Harari, because Major Pesach had not mentioned any such arrangement.

'The plan only came up after you left Tel-Aviv,' Karlim explained. 'You will be escorted to Nuremberg, and from there you will fly to Israel by private jet.'

But Harari's astonishment only increased when Karlim steered the conversation to the immediate escape plans from East Berlin: the two-hundred-mile trip by car to Sonneberg, which he considered the riskiest part of the venture. In the half hour after Professor Goldman's disappearance, the KGB and the STASI would set up roadblocks all over the country. They would stop and search every single vehicle travelling in the direction of the border on the Autobahn through Brandenburg.

'First of all, they will alert the checkpoints in Berlin, but you will be travelling south, towards Leipzig, bound for Czechoslovakia, over a good two-thirds of the trip. For a while, at least, no one would think of looking for you on that road.' He paused for a moment, then added emphatically, 'but it is unlikely that the STASI would dare to challenge a Soviet general, travelling in uniform, with full escort, on urgent official business . . .'

Darit's chin dropped. Harari stared at Karlim blankly.

'You mean, Goldman – a Soviet general?'

'A KGB general, just to be on the safe side,' Karlim replied flatly. 'Why not? He is a Russian, isn't he? At one time he even served in the Red Army. Nobody in this servile country will have the guts to hinder him, certainly not one of those hick East German commanders. Naturally, you will all be issued the appropriate official documents and badges.'

'KGB?'

'Nearly as good as the originals.'

Captain Harari was flabbergasted. Karlim continued evenly. 'You will have an authentic Russian Dnepr motorcycle. Red Army Lieutenant Jorv Amran will use it to ride in front of the limousine, which will be flying the staff flag.

You – a captain – should be the driver. Posing as a major, Ariel Cohen can be the general's adjutant, and Doctor Efrati —' he paused to make a complimentary bow to Darit. 'You will most probably be the prettiest secretary a Soviet general could wish for, travelling likewise in uniform.'

Gradually the magnitude of Karlim's suggestion began to dawn on Harari. It was a fantastic idea indeed, vastly increasing their chances of reaching Sonneberg safely. Or, at least, as far as the hunting lodge which belonged to Martin Drexler. Once they got there, they would be able to remove Jacques Moura's special equipment from the Mercedes.

'Where will we get the Soviet uniforms from?' he asked.

'You – nowhere. I have already got them.' Karlim looked at Harari. 'What do you think of my plan?' he asked eagerly. 'Major Pesach approves it.'

Harari slapped him on the back. 'Well, a man can only be killed once,' he retorted. 'Whether it happens when one is in plain clothes, or in uniform, it wouldn't make any difference.'

Professor Goldman's arrival in East Berlin was a most cordial event. The reception committee waiting to greet him consisted of the Deputy Minister of Cultural Affairs, the Chairman of the Academy of Sciences, a high-ranking member of the local Politburo, the First Secretary of the Soviet Embassy, a conglomeration of East German scientists, news reporters, and the traditional little girl in colourful national dress. Ignoring all the dignitaries towering over her, the pretty, blonde child skipped right up to the professor and gave him a bunch of red roses, then waited to receive a customary kiss upon her cheek in return. But when Goldman raised her up, she slipped a small metal tube into his hand and whispered the word, 'Pesach.'

Professor Goldman was astounded, but managed to preserve his smiling countenance. This is really incredible, he thought, again marvelling at Israeli ingenuity. Major

Pesach's agents had contacted him in Moscow, in the Romanian capital, and now again here in Berlin, the moment he set foot on East German soil.

His KGB escort, Captain Igor Malcev, only smiled jovially, patted the little girl's face and courteously took the flowers from Goldman. He then stood right next to him, serenely, like a bridegroom waiting for his bride. His air of pious solicitude almost caused Goldman to laugh aloud. A KGB captain with roses.

The professor wondered if the child was Jewish, but he doubted it. She was too blonde, too blue-eyed and so typically Nordic.

Pretending to get a handkerchief out of his pocket, he managed to hide what he now recognised was a small capsule. It contained a laconic message which he later read in the privacy of his bathroom, and destroyed immediately afterwards.

Next Friday between 11.00 and 11.30 a.m.
S-Bahn station, Wuhlheide Pioneer Park.

Now it was Monday. Tuesday had been kept free of official engagements. On Wednesday, Thursday and Friday, he had meetings scheduled at the Academy of Sciences. He decided that his best chance to get away from Malcev would come while they were inside the Academy complex. Apparently the Israelis were aware of this, because they had chosen the last day of the scientific gathering, probably thinking that the two previous days should help to build up Malcev's confidence and relax his vigilance.

After the welcoming ceremony in the airport lounge, the two men were driven to a government guest house in Pankow-Heinesdorf, a former noble palace in a magnificent park, converted into luxurious apartments for visiting foreign dignitaries. The flats were completely self-contained. Jakov Abramovich Goldman was allocated a beautifully appointed three-room suite, lavishly furnished with valuable paintings, Oriental carpets, and a marble bathroom. Captain Malcev had to be content with a room in the adjacent officers' quarters. No foreign visitor needed an escort inside the complex. The entire length of the road leading to the guest house had been proclaimed 'off limits' to ordinary mortals, and along the walled perimeter, 'Vopos' patrolled, with machine guns and trained dogs.

In a sense, Professor Goldman did not mind residing in this gilded prison, which did at least afford him some privacy. He was certain that, had he been booked into an hotel, Igor Malcev would have moved right in with him, in the double bed, swallowing the key for the night. Throughout the voyage the KGB captain had been doing his utmost to 'assist' Goldman in every possible manner.

As would be expected, the guest house accommodated many interesting personalities. Over dinner, Professor Goldman was introduced to the North Korean Minister of Commerce, to the Lao-Dong Party secretary of Hanoi, to the bearded director of the Bank of Cuba, who merrily boasted that he was on his seventh visit to East Germany. Probably his seventh milking-trip, Goldman commented inwardly. The Cubans were also frequent visitors to Moscow, where ordinary citizens would refer to them as the milkmen – who did not deliver milk, but instead would come to milk the USSR.

Goldman also exchanged a brief conversation with an Arab dignitary from Syria, who turned out to be Yasser Arafat's brother. He grasped Goldman's hand in both palms with genuine Oriental fervour, naturally ignorant of the fact that the professor was Jewish. His enthusiasm was a homage to the Soviet scientist, who had worked on the SAM missiles now in Syrian possession. The notion occurred to Goldman that perhaps in a few days' time they would be neighbours, and his erstwhile friend would be spitting curses in Goldman's direction.

He greatly enjoyed the situation.

Both Monday and Tuesday mornings were spent with visits and courtesy calls. They lunched at the Soviet Embassy, a gigantic complex of which – both Goldman and

Malcev knew – only a tiny segment served as a diplomatic mission. The rest of the monolithic construction housed various offices concerned exclusively with non-socialist affairs.

The embassy car drove them to the monument erected in commemoration to the twenty thousand Russian soldiers who had fallen in the battle of Berlin, four thousand eight hundred of whom now rested in five giant common tombs.

After a few more hours spent sightseeing there was a luncheon with the Chairman of the Academy and an official dinner with the SED Party Secretary. The first two days passed quickly. On Wednesday morning the lecture sessions at the Academy began. By now bored to death, Captain Malcev occupied a vacant chair in the uppermost row of seats in the vast lecture hall. Occasionally he would listen to the discourse, but most of the time he immersed himself in the pages of the *Trud* or *Pravda*. Professor Goldman's opinion of the latter newspaper was one shared by most Russian Jews, that the only truth contained in it was the three words: 'Price Five Kopeks.'

Whenever Goldman went out to the bar, Malcev was there, joining him for a coffee or a sandwich, tailing him like a good dog. Goldman only smiled at his tenacity.

On Thursday afternoon, the day before his planned departure from the communist world, Professor Goldman and Captain Malcev went for a quiet stroll to visit the historical site, the 'Führerbunker' on Otto Grotewohl street – once called Wilhelmstrasse. Of Hitler's Reichskanzlei, nothing now remained, and now only a few derelict stones marked the former site of the famous Hotel Adlon. The Nazi foreign ministry under Ribbentrop had also been demolished. Of the former Third Reich edifices, only Goebbels' Ministry of Propaganda still stood, on the Ernst Thaelman Platz. Completely restored, the building now housed the East German National Council – an appropriate residence for the state elders, the professor reflected. After all, in a sense they were doing the same sort of job, only under different colours.

During the walk, Captain Malcev indulged him in patriotic reminiscences and talked incessantly of the great battles in which his father had participated. He had won the highest decoration: Hero of the Soviet Union. The professor did not pay much attention to Malcev's eulogies, but tried to steer their apparently aimless walk along the streets he intended to take the next day to get to the S-Bahn station on Karl Marx Platz. Pausing here and there to look in shop windows, the good KGB captain made quite a few remarks about the damned locals, who generally enjoyed a much better lifestyle than their Soviet compatriots at home.

'This is what we were bled white for in the war, Jakov Abramovich,' Malcev grumbled. 'So that our socialist brothers can wear fancy Western dress, sit in flashy bars and dance to decadent Western rock 'n' roll.' His statement caught Goldman somewhat by surprise; Malcev did sound genuinely indignant. 'It is not right,' he continued scornfully. 'Colour TVs, washing machines, hi-fi equipment, motorcycles . . . At home one must wait for months before receiving a colour TV, for which one has had to pay in advance. What a world to live in.'

Professor Goldman laughed before admonishing him.

'Comrade Malcev, if I didn't know better, I'd say you are broadcasting subversive propaganda.'

Igor Malcev frowned, pursed his lips and cast a sideways glance at Goldman, trying to decide whether the professor was being sarcastic, or was only amused.

'Is it not true that the Russian people deprive themselves so that our allies may be content and suffer no hardship? We bear the entire cost of their defence and keep their industries going with our raw materials and fuel. Of course they are able to produce luxury goods.' Looking at Goldman, he added conspiratorailly, 'between ourselves, Jakov Abramovich, I don't trust the Germans one bit. But *we* are friends, aren't we?'

'I certainly hope so,' the professor replied with pretended conviction. 'Anyway, we seem to have been having a good time since Bucharest, Captain Malcev.' They had long since moved beyond Malcev's initial 'Intourist Guide' ploy. Now they understood each other's roles very well.

'Why not call me Igor?'

'*Ochen Kharashoh* – Igor, then,' Goldman acquiesced, but thought to himself: You wouldn't hesitate to have me shot if it would gain you a major's star, friend Igor. 'I am not particularly fond of Germans myself,' he added aloud.

'Of course, your Jewish ancestry,' Malcev commented with understanding. 'Riga, Poltava and Babi-Yar.'

'Where the Nazis killed my brother and his wife.'

'Sad, very sad,' the captain added sympathetically.

Just as they were crossing the Karl Marx Platz, Professor Goldman, acting on a sudden inspiration, suggested that they take a trip on the S-Bahn to the suburb of Koepenick, one station further down the line from Wuhlheide. He thought this would be an ideal way to familiarise himself with the route, thus avoiding any delays tomorrow. 'I read somewhere about some excellent little taverns there where one may dine cheaply.'

Malcev had nothing against the excursion. Their afternoon was free. While he went to buy the tickets, Goldman memorised the time-table, and decided he should try to get the 11.15 train the following day.

The trip was a pleasant one, except for the 'slightly upset stomach' Goldman began to complain about shortly after the meal. 'I fear that our lunch was a little too rich for my digestion,' he excused himself, and went to the lavatory. Immediately gripped by a similar urge, Igor Malcev followed him. Laughing to himself, the professor decided to play him along. Throughout the afternoon he repeatedly made his excuses, until at last Malcev became tired of running after him.

On the Friday morning, just before the third session at the Academy was due to begin, Goldman drew the Chairman aside and politely informed him of his indisposition, excusing himself beforehand for the recurring necessity to leave the lecture hall. Every now and then he

127

went to the toilet and noted with satisfaction that Malcev could no longer be bothered to tail him, and now remained in his seat.

Shortly after a quarter to eleven, the professor left the conference hall for the fourth time. The discussion on his lecture continued, but after some ten minutes had elapsed, Captain Malcev clambered to his feet and went to look for Goldman, who he thought might be really unwell. He could not find him either in the lavatory or in the bar. Soon he became restless. He checked the lounge, enquired in the library and at the secretary's office, then hurried downstairs to the cloakroom. The professor's hat and overcoat were there, and Malcev heaved a sigh of relief. Goldman had to be somewhere in the building, perhaps talking to a colleague in a private office, or in one of the laboratories. After another half hour had elapsed, however, he decided to page Goldman over the intercom.

He waited in vain for a response.

One after another his self-comforting reasons for Goldman's absence crumbled, and cold fear clutched at his guts. Now perspiring profusely, his temples throbbing, he rushed back to the entrance hall. 'Yes, I think Professor Goldman went out twenty minutes ago,' the receptionist told him. 'He asked me for the address of the nearest pharmacy.'

Renewed relief.

'Without his overcoat?' Malcev asked.

'I found that rather odd, myself,' the receptionist replied. Then, seeing Malcev's apparent concern, she added consolingly, 'it is not particularly cold outside, and the pharmacy is only two doors away.'

Once again Igor Malcev tried to reassure himself. Goldman had probably decided to get himself some medicine after all. It must have been truly depressing to attend an important meeting with dodgy bowels. He glanced at his watch and felt his body give way to another fit of cold shivers. It was almost eleven-thirty. The professor had been absent for over half an hour. His previous consternation returned – only stronger now.

Malcev bolted down the wide staircase and hurried out to the pharmacy. No, they had not served anyone this morning who answered Goldman's description.

In another local pharmacy the answer was the same.

Close to desperation, the captain returned to the Academy. His last hope collapsed. Goldman had not returned.

Wild alternatives flooded his mind. A chance accident . . . hit by a car . . . sudden heart attack . . . Goldman had a heart condition. Accumulated stress could have triggered it.

Taken to hospital. Kidnapped by the CIA.

Fled to West Berlin. *Defected*.

The receptionist was most cooperative. A few quick phone calls revealed that Goldman had not been involved in a road accident, and was not in hospital. Neither had he returned to the guest house.

Captain Igor Malcev felt his world crashing down on him.

11.45 A.M. Goldman had been absent for one hour.

How much can happen in one hour? Until an hour ago, Malcev had been a contented man. The trip with Goldman had been a smooth affair of pompous receptions, lavish luncheons and dinners, sightseeing tours in chauffeur-driven limousines, accommodation in luxury hotels, all paid for by the host governments. Malcev's daily allowance from Mother Russia had therefore been available to be converted into fine suits, shoes and exciting electronic gadgets, hard to come by at home. And everything duty-free, because when it came to the luggage of KGB officers, all formalities were waived. Professor Goldman had been an excellent ward, pleasant to travel with, a good conversationalist, and as good-natured as a lamb. Malcev's assignment had seemed free of problems. Nevertheless, he had followed his orders to the letter and had stuck to the professor wherever he went. Apparently Goldman had not minded their close relationship – not even the sharing of hotel suites. Malcev had been happy until an hour ago. He appreciated the way the Romanian and Czech authorities had jumped to attend his slightest whim. An active KGB officer on an official trip was a king of kings in the fellow socialist countries.

He could not imagine that Goldman's apparent timidity and keen observance of all the rules, his fervently displayed patriotism, had been performed only to lull him into a false sense of security.

He was a fool. And when he realised that the professor had most likely defected, Malcev fell into a kind of stupor of fear. He had failed. Failed miserably, and it would not be forgiven. In the KGB there was no atonement. At best he would be demoted and dispatched to some Godforsaken post in Sibera. At worst . . . *Bozhe moy*, he found himself using God's name for the first time in his adult life. He did not even wish to think of the worst. He closed his mind to any of the possible alternatives.

For a while he strolled aimlessly around the streets, and in his ever-increasing despair he even toyed with the idea of defecting himself. His knowledge of KGB affairs was extensive, could easily be turned into hard cash and a new identity in the West. But soon he abandoned such treacherous thoughts. He did not feel like becoming a traitor, losing his wife and two young sons . . . What would be their lot in the neighbourhood, in school? The traitor's wife and children. They'd be thrown out of the comfortable apartment. Elena would lose her job.

He did not want to be shot, either.

Perhaps the worst could still be avoided. Perhaps Goldman would be stopped at the border. The East German frontiers were nearly impregnable – especially to an elderly scholar, inexperienced and unaccustomed to physical strain, and with a bad heart. There was yet hope . . .

But perhaps Goldman had helpers. The CIA, British Intelligence.

If the frontier guards arrested Goldman, his own punishment would be milder. Perhaps a relocation without demotion. After all, Stalin and Beria were no longer around. KGB chief Andropov was neither cruel nor inconsiderate.

Wiping his forehead with trembling fingers, he dialled the Soviet Embassy in East Berlin and reported what had happened. He was immediately put through to Major General Pavel Podgorski, the head of the local KGB, who ordered Malcev to report in immediately. The captain felt himself shrivelling up, but went to his doom all the same.

Professor Goldman's first encounter with the Israeli team looked like a perfectly casual event. He left the S-Bahn station and saw the black Mercedes parked with several people sitting inside. Harari recognised the professor instantly, and Ariel Cohen, sitting in the rear, opened the door for him. '*Shalom*, Professor Goldman.'

Goldman shrank back in terror. The occupants of the limousine were all wearing the uniforms of the Soviet security forces, and the unexpected sight nearly paralysed him.

Seeing Goldman's consternation, Darit said quietly, 'please don't be surprised, Professor Goldman. These Soviet uniforms are going to provide the safest way to reach the border unhindered.'

Professor Goldman's relief was plainly visible. The colour returned to his cheeks and he sighed as he sat down beside Ariel. 'I thought I had run straight into a trap.'

Harari uttered a soft chuckle. 'Not even the KGB works that fast, Professor.'

He started the car immediately, and soon they were heading towards the Dresden highway. 'What a brilliant idea!' the professor commented, indicating the immaculate uniforms. Ariel Cohen was dressed as a major; in front, Harari and Darit were a KGB captain and lieutenant respectively.

'You must get changed as well, Professor,' Darit told him lightly. 'You are going to be our General. If we run into a roadblock, you must do all the talking – in Russian.'

Goldman shook his head. 'Sometimes talking is not enough. Sometimes one has to show one's credentials,' he replied quietly.

Harari turned to Darit. 'Would you hand the professor his credentials?'

Goldman took the small folder. Speechlessly he stared at its contents.

Identity card. State Security clearance documents. Photo. Seal . . . General Sergei Alexeievich Morozov, KGB Moscow.

'You Israelis aren't scared of anything, are you?' he said with genuine admiration in his voice.

'We have learned from long experience that bold actions are half a victory,' Harari replied. Darit then pointed at the uniform that hung from a window hook beside Ariel.

'How am I going to change with you present, Doctor Efrati?' Goldman asked with a faintly nervous laugh.

'Please call me Darit, if you don't mind. I will look straight ahead, if it concerns you.' She smiled gently.

Helped by Ariel, the professor changed into the general's uniform, which was generously adorned with orders of bravery and service. 'Well, I was once in the Red Army engineering corps, though not at the rank of general,' he commented. Suddenly he exclaimed at the sight of a Red Army lieutenant, armed with a machine gun, riding a motorcycle just in front of the car. 'Who is he?'

'Our fourth companion. Lieutenant Jorv Amran,' Harari told him cheerfully. 'His rank is real, only the uniform is different.'

'Why the motorcycle?'

'We thought it would be more impressive for a general to travel in this manner,' Darit told him.

'Very clever. You have planned this excellently. Not one detail had been overlooked. Now, may I ask where we are going?'

'Certainly,' Ariel Cohen answered him. 'To a place

called Sonneberg, south of Leipzig, on the West German frontier.'

'Are we going to climb fences in Soviet uniforms?' Goldman said with a chuckle. 'It would be rather funny.'

'No, no,' Ariel protested. 'We are going to get across the border underground. Like rabbits. We have a warren. All that needs to be done now is for us to make the run.'

'Have you dug a tunnel?' Goldman wondered.

'No. Sonneberg is a deserted coal mine,' Cohen explained. For the next twenty minutes Harari and Cohen related the plan in some detail. After a moment's silence, while he reflected on the plan, the professor's reaction came in the form of the first lines of the familiar Hebrew prayer.

'*Shma Yisroel Adonai Elohenu Adonai Echod . . .*'

8

If Captain Igor Malcev still hoped for a happy solution to his predicament, Major General Pavel Podgorski, the head of the KGB East Berlin office, did not entertain similar sentiments. He had come across defectors before, all of them excellent, trusted comrades with unblemished records, coming from the working class and educated by the Communist Party. Usually they were scholars, élite sportsmen and artists upon whom the party bestowed the highest decorations and rarest benefits. Members of the Red Army had also defected to the decadent capitalist West; a couple of pilots, marine officers, and even the odd KGB functionary. All were capable of causing immense damage to the USSR.

Now Professor Jakov Abramovich Goldman, an elderly scholar, who lived with honour and in comfort in Moscow. What could he possibly expect to gain by spending his remaining years in the West?

Money? Fame? He had always been well looked after in Russia, and he was famous enough. Why this sudden turnaround in the autumn of his life? As a person, he had seemed rather insignificant, even simple. Yet he was more perilous than all the others who had fled before him. Traitors who defected to the West almost always took with them a few minor confidentialities: perhaps something like the names of a few KGB plants in Europe or America. But Goldman was carrying with him the entire Soviet SAM system. He must be stopped.

Ten minutes after Malcev's report had been received, the sophisticated KGB apparatus had shunted into top gear, concentrating on 'Case Goldman'; for the time being everything else was set aside. The East German MFS had been put on red alert. The computers of the STASI began to compile information on all foreign visitors who had checked out of their hotels or campsites on Friday morning, shortly before, or immediately after, Goldman's disappearance. KGB Major General Podgorski did not even consider the possibility that the professor had acted without the aid of foreign helpers.

The resulting 268 names, complete with all the relevant personal data, were then run through a second procedure which filtered out the less likely subjects: elderly couples, parents with children, minors, package tour travellers, and all tourists who had by late Friday morning legitimately departed from East Berlin.

All visa applications with photos were processed and compared with exit papers. By the end of this exhaustive elimination process they were left with the files of just four individuals who had not yet left East Germany, although they had checked out of their hotels on the same morning and had not yet registered themselves anywhere else.

A young French couple from Paris. A Libyan businessman and a Hungarian tourist; the last two had been travelling alone, but they had booked into the same hotel and had both checked out on the same morning – Friday. Major General Podgorski's nose smelled a rat.

Hungarian tourists seldom travelled alone. Indeed, very seldom. And this one had not come directly from Hungary either, but from Vienna. He had also been in France.

France – Paris? Like the French couple?

Major General Podgorski had by now summoned Colonel Ivan Sedov, his liaison officer with the MFS, and his second-in-command, Major Riumin. Also ordered to attend the first meeting were Lt General Gerhard Stutz, the head of the STASI, with his adjutant Colonel Hans Meinecke. They scanned the files with expert eyes. Four yellow folders were spread open side by side upon the desk. More odd coincidences caught his attention. The Hungarian and the Libyan had entered East Germany by train from Czechoslovakia. The same train! The Libyan had booked into the Hotel Grunewald on schedule; the Hungarian had chosen the same hotel, but nearly sixteen hours later. Obviously he had spent a day somewhere else, somewhere between the border and Berlin. Where?

Podgorski looked straight at Lt General Gerhard Stutz, his East German counterpart, and said with gravity, 'Comrade, find out what the Hungarian was doing during those sixteen hours, and very soon you will probably have a resident agent in your hands.'

Within twenty minutes the KGB received the official Hungarian response to their urgent telex. No passport of the given particulars had ever been issued by the Ministry of the Interior. The given number did not exist. The passport was a forgery.

Major General Podgorski commented wryly, 'we have our first Enemy Agent.'

Colonel Muammar Muhammad Al Gaddafi had also been most cooperative. By two o'clock on the same afternoon the suspected Libyan businessman had also been unmasked as a spy, and Podgorski had got his Agent Number Two.

'We need not even bother with the French couple,' he told General Stutz. 'It could take days.'

'We do have one communist comrade in the Ministry of the Interior who would be willing to help,' Colonel Sedov ventured. 'Also Comrade Sobirev, at the Embassy.'

Major General Podgorski only waved an impatient hand. 'What for? They are obviously members of the same team.'

'The CIA again?' General Stutz asked quietly.

Podgorski shrugged. 'CIA, CIC, Deuxième Bureau, British Intelligence Service, German BND . . . We'll find out when we capture them. Have the STASI flash the registration number of the black Mercedes to every checkpoint between here and the border.'

'It has already been done, Comrade Podgorski,' the East German general replied smugly.

'Yes, your German efficiency,' Podgorski answered with a thin smile.

'It should not be difficult to trace the car,' Stutz went on, immensely content that the initial surveillance of Professor Goldman had not been entrusted to the STASI, although he anticipated more heated encounters with the KGB chief if the defector was not found. Naturally the Russians would blame the East Germans. They would yell about loose controls, slack vigilance, insufficient security measures, leaky roadblocks. It had always been so. The KGB never made mistakes, only the allies did.

Major General Podgorski suggested that hourly meetings be set up to discuss subsequent developments. The professor's photograph was shown every hour on the TV news, but, so far at least, the word 'defection' was not to be mentioned. The announcer spoke of possible abduction by enemy agents, and a reward of fifty thousand Ostmarks was offered to anyone able to furnish decisive information on his whereabouts. Later newscasts also featured the enlarged photos of Harari, Amran, Cohen and Dr Efrati.

The first part of the long drive was uneventful. Goldman and the Israelis talked about their respective past experiences, and of Israel, which the elderly scholar only knew from what he could occasionally learn by tuning into Radio Jerusalem, and even that only in the privacy of his apartment.

'I know that you are turning the Negev desert into a veritable Garden of Eden,' he said to Cohen. 'It must be a monumental undertaking.'

'And one of the many reasons why the Arabs are so envious of us,' Ariel answered. 'We are transforming the arid wastelands of millennia into fertile pastures and orchards, and have done more in thirty years than the Arabs had achieved in centuries.'

'But, in the end, it is the Negev that will be Israel's salvation. A nation which can feed itself in that part of the world will be the one to triumph ultimately,' said the professor, the pride obvious in his voice.

Harari cut in without turning round. 'Yes. Even so, the Arabs seem to have the habit of doing just the opposite. They prefer turning cities and orchards into deserts, then go raving about their bad luck and blame the Zionists.'

Darit, who had been listening for a while, added, 'the Arabs will never progress the way Israel does, because twentieth-century developments no longer tally with the credo laid down in the Koran. Look at the Ayatollah Khomeini – a medieval despot cast abroad in the missile age. He is slaughtering his own people by the thousand. Just imagine what he would to others.'

'I don't think the Arabs will ever make peace with Israel,' Professor Goldman remarked with a tinge of irony.

'We know,' Harari answered. 'They seem unable to make peace, having so many different sectarian groups, each with a leader possessed by his own ideas and illusions. If one of them agrees to something, the others won't.'

'Egypt has decided to opt for peace,' Darit reminded him. 'Others might follow.'

'Perhaps Jordan – yes,' Harari agreed. 'But Syria must be beaten decisively before they will come to terms. Others who live far from Israel have nothing to lose by continuing to be aggressive.'

'Do you think there'll be another war in Syria?'

'It is inevitable. When Assad thinks that he has acquired enough Soviet hardware, he'll give it another try.'

They came to a roadsign warning of a sharp right turn.

Riding the Dnepr some twenty yards ahead of the Mercedes, Jorv leaned into a bend and took it at speed, but

Harari slowed the car down to fifty. Immediately after the bend stood a large, portable sign: *Achtung. Polizei. HALT.*

A roadblock.

Cleverly placed behind the bend and not visible from any distance. Fifty yards further on, coils of barbed wire barred the highway; there was a row of tyre-traps studded with needle-sharp steel cones. At the side of the road an armoured car loomed with its heavy machine gun pointing down and the gunner ready. On either side of the tarmac, troops of the Volksarmee stood rigidly, wielding Kalashnikovs, forefingers clamped on the triggers.

'Here we go,' Harari spoke tersely. Cohen uttered a half-hearted sound of consternation and Darit's fingers clamped on Hadar's arm.

In front of them, Amran came to a skidding stop, planted his feet firmly on the asphalt and swung his machine gun round to rest against his chest. His eyes were hard as jade, but his face betrayed no emotion at all. It showed only indifference to what must have been dreary routine to a Red Army officer. But he checked the place and his mind whirled like a computer, calculating chances, printing the final result – how many of them could he kill before succumbing himself.

The limousine rolled to a smooth halt. Harari lowered the powered window. His eyes closed to slits. 'East Germans,' he commented in a low voice. Goldman said in a calm, balanced tone, 'Don't worry. I think I can handle them.'

A close-cropped, lean captain came towards the car, impeccably dressed and carrying about him an aura of rigid authority which, however, rapidly diminished at the sight of the senior staff flag flying from the bonnet.

Recognising the Soviet uniforms, the last vestige of his authority collapsed into a kind of embarrassed indecisiveness. He saluted, bent down and gave the interior a peremptory glance, saw the glittering insignia of a full KGB general on Goldman's uniform, stepped back, and froze to rigid attention. He cleared his throat, trying to gain a little time while contemplating how to proceed. He swallowed and opted for playing it safe.

'Hauptman Kurt Wiesinger of the Dzerzhinski Brigade reporting, Comrade General,' he rasped, addressing Goldman, who was sitting stony-faced next to a Red Army major, obviously the general's adjutant. The East German captain could speak Russian well, but now found himself searching for words, not wishing to be impolite. He looked quite miserable, as if complaining inwardly: Why did this have to happen to me?

Adin Karlim's idea seemed to be paying dividends.

The captain muttered a few words of apology for the inconvenience, but he had his orders. He wanted to say something else, but the general's eyes transfixed him. '*Tovarishch, Kapitan.*' Goldman spoke in a cold, emotionless voice which nevertheless sounded menacing. 'You surely know what the words *Komitet Gosudarstvennoi Bezhopanosti* stand for?'

The East German captain swallowed again and uttered a sound of discomfort. He knew too well the meaning of those three words: KGB, and all it stood for.

'Certainly, Comrade General —'

'Then you should also know that we do not like losing time.'

'Comrade General, I am only doing . . .'

'Your duty,' Goldman finished for him. 'So are we.' He glanced at his wristwatch and added calmly, 'Captain, it would normally take you about two minutes to have the road cleared. I am giving you exactly one minute.'

Feeling hot and cold at the same time, the captain stepped back and saluted for the third time, then spun on his heels and shouted a guttural command.

'*Strasse freigeben! Schnell!*'

His soldiers jerked into action. Shouldering their guns, they hurried to open the way. The professor must be a damned good poker player, Harari complimented inwardly. In a few seconds the road was free. Amran kicked his motor and Harari shifted the gears on the Mercedes.

'Attention!' Captain Wiesinger commanded. 'Present arms!' He saluted again.

'He's quite smart about it,' Harari thought. 'Seeing us off in style.'

Goldman responded with a casual salute. The limousine gathered speed and the roadblock receded into the distance.

Ariel dabbed at his perspiring face and heaved a prolonged sigh of relief.

'Were you scared, Ariel?' Hadar asked him.

'Yes, scared enough,' Cohen confessed earnestly. 'These pseudo-Nazis always give me the creeps.'

Harari laughed softly. 'I don't know who was more scared, you or the East German captain.'

'Probably the unfortunate captain,' the professor interposed mildly.

'Why unfortunate?' Darit queried.

'Because he has just failed miserably, and the KGB never forigves. He had been told to look for Jakov Abramovich Goldman, a Russian defector, and instead got himself a KGB general. Sooner or later his blunder shall be known. You see, the general's star is impressive enough, but the word KGB can work wonders in this part of the world. The captain was scared. He wanted to play it safe and he lost. That is communism. Everyone is scared of everyone in a higher position.' He paused for a moment, then added admiringly, 'this Lieutenant Karlim of yours must be a brilliantly inventive man.'

'He is an experienced agent, that's all,' Harari replied evenly.

'Were you not even a little concerned, Professor?' Darit asked.

Goldman put out his arm. 'Do you want to check my pulse? A hundred or so over ninety. No more.'

'You were marvellous at handling the situation. Perhaps somewhere inside you there is a great actor dying to get out.'

'Everybody is an actor, Darit. I did not really risk

141

anything . . . You see, you were born and bred a free citizen of a mighty little nation, and it might be difficult for you to understand, or even imagine, everyday life behind the Iron Curtain. Of course, the Israelis also have enemies. Very dangerous enemies, and sometimes you must be scared. But only of your enemies. In my country – I hope that soon I may call it my former country – we must be afraid of our superiors, our subalterns, the caretaker of the house we live in, the waiter at the restaurant we lunch at, the electrician, the plumber, our neighbours. In many cases we must be afraid even of our best friends. The KGB has half a million active members and twenty million part-time informers, infiltrating every level of the society. Until today, I was a part of this system of fear. I have lived in it all my life, and I know it well. The East German captain lives in a similar system, so it was not difficult to gauge his reaction.'

When questioned, an employee at the S-Bahn ticket counter on the Karl Marx Platz thought he had seen Goldman; a well-dressed, elderly man, walking about without an overcoat and hat, which looked odd, given that the weather had turned cold again. He had asked for a ticket to Wuhlheide; his Russian accent was pronounced.

The search thus concentrated in the Wuhlheide area.

The prospect of a generous reward also stirred the memory of a university student. Alighting at the same station, he claimed to have seen the elderly man without an overcoat get into a black Mercedes limousine which already had several people inside, among them a woman. The student thought the occupants of the car were Russian officers in uniform. He seemed quite certain on that point.

This Russian angle gave the search renewed impetus. It did not take long for the KGB experts to deduce what had happened and understand the agents' *modus operandi*. The checkpoints and roadblocks were alerted to this new development.

When STASI Captain Wiesinger received the telex about a team of enemy agents and the fugitive Russian scientists travelling south-west in a black Mercedes car, masquerading as Soviet officers, he almost fainted.

The limousine was traced to Dresden, where a highway patrol had seen it speeding towards Karl Marx Stadt. A policeman directing traffic around roadworks near Neustadt also remembered the Soviet staff car and the Red Army lieutenant riding a motorcycle in front of it. He had stopped the other traffic in order to give precedence to the Russians.

In the meantime, the STASI had received Captain Wiesinger's report regarding a KGB general and his escort, who had passed through his roadblock twelve miles before Saalfeld, near the township of Poesneck along highway 281. Lt General Stutz did not bother to ask why the captain in charge hadn't examined the Russians' documents. East German police and military were not permitted to challenge members of the Red Army.

That black Mercedes limousine . . .

Which had not turned up either in the frontier town of Eisfeld, or at the Neuhaus roadblock, twelve miles to the north.

The officers studied the map. The only other possible route from highway 281 led from Piesau to Sonneberg. There were no other roads, not even dirt roads. Nor were there any viable border crossings in the Sonneberg triangle. The agents with Goldman seemed to be heading straight into a dead end.

'Is there anything special about the Sonneberg region?' a drawn-faced Major General Podgorski asked his East German colleague.

'Nothing that I know of,' Lt General Stutz replied with a puzzled expression. 'We exercise the usual security measures within the two-mile frontier-zone facing West Germany. It is a *Sperrgebiet*.'

But Podgorski had his reservations.

'There has to be something special about Sonneberg,' he remarked thoughtfully. 'Those agents are experts. They would never run into a stupid trap. I am convinced that Goldman's defection has been thoroughly prepared.' He glanced up from the map. 'Flash a special alert to Sonneberg.' He turned to Colonel Sedov. 'Have a helicopter ready, Colonel. You and Major Riumin are going to Sonneberg to work with the local STASI.'

When Podgorski was called to the direct line to Moscow, he felt a dull sense of foreboding about the music he was sure he was about to hear. He poured himself a generous glass of Stolichnaya and downed it in one long gulp. He did not appreciate direct calls from Moscow. They were never pleasant.

'It's General Sherbakov,' his adjutant reported, almost in a whisper. Podgorski thought to himself, there goes my long-awaited Great October Revolution decoration. In any case, he hoped that it would only be his decoration to go. Whenever a high-ranking member of the KGB fell into disgrace, someone else would climb up a grade.

His superior in Moscow skipped all the usual preliminaries and came to the point straightaway. 'Podgorski,' Sherbakov rasped, omitting both rank and 'comrade'. 'It is your responsibility to recover Jakov Abramovich Goldman, or his corpse. I presume you do know something of the information he is carrying?'

'I do, Comrade General,' Podgorski answered glumly. Of course he knew what the renegade professor was taking away – the entire Soviet surface-to-air missile system. 'We are doing our best to stop him.'

'You'll have to do a great deal more than your best.'

'I understand that, Comrade General. The entire Western frontier is on first-grade alert. The Felix Dzerzhinski brigade is on the move and roadblocks are being set up on every highway.'

'Being?' Sherbakov asked sardonically. 'What about the secondary roads? Gravel roads? Country dirt roads? What measures have you taken to seal those off?'

'All communications to the frontier have been blocked.'

There was a moment's silence, after which Sherbakov asked gruffly, 'where is that bloody idiot?'

'Igor Malcev?'

'Who else?'

'In custody, at the Embassy.'

'*Kharashoh* – put him on the next plane to Moscow.'

'He says he does not feel well, Comrade General.'

Sherbakov chuckled. 'I would not feel well in his skin, the bloody fool. His only hope for salvation rests with the quick recovery of Goldman.'

'Malcev realises that only too well,' General Podgorski replied, then added with a sudden surge of magnanimity, 'at least he was not in on the plot, or else he would have defected too.'

'Just don't let anything happen to him.'

'Oh, no – he is being held under guard.'

'Well, get on with the work. I want frequent reports. Details,' Sherbakov concluded.

'Certainly, if you so desire, Comrade General.'

'It is not I who so desire, but Comrade Andropov, and he is feeling extremely sour. He told me he has Marshal Ustinov and half a dozen generals on his back, all pressing for the elimination of Goldman.'

Young Kurt Drexler was watching TV and only by chance saw the newsreel featuring the pictures of four Imperialist agents who may have kidnapped a highly revered Russian scholar. The photos of the wanted persons were held on the screen for a full thirty seconds. Kurt almost fell off his chair.

There was no doubt. One of the wanted agents was the stranger he had briefly encountered here at home, in the hall. That man had definitely been the one who came to visit his grandfather a couple of days ago.

The same man, Kurt was certain.

He dashed to the door and yanked it open. '*Mutti*,' he called excitedly. '*Komm schnell!*' There was no response, then Kurt remembered that his mother had gone out shopping.

His father was still at the office, and Grandpa was probably taking a nap.

The screen still projected the pictures and the announcer's voice droned on.

'. . . reason to believe that the fugitives have already passed Karl Marx Stadt, heading south-west, perhaps posing as officers of the Red Army. They are armed and should be considered dangerous. The black Mercedes limousine . . .'

He turned off the set and hurried downstairs.

What should he do? Perhaps, given his help, the agents would be arrested. Were they not constantly being reminded in school, in the youth organisation, of the necessity of being forever alert? Because the enemies of socialism were relentlessly trying to destroy the DDR.

He might be decorated, featured in the newspapers as a prime example of communist youth. He would pass his school exams more easily, and of course, there was also the reward.

Twenty thousand Ostmarks – a year's wages for his father.

There was no time to waste.

Kurt Drexler did not stop to consider the possible consequences for his family. The good of the fatherland and the party came before any other consideration.

His face was flushed and the heat of excitement burned inside him as he picked up the phone and, with unsteady fingers, dialled the number of a classmate. Hans's father was a police sergeant. He would know what to do next.

Fifteen minutes later a dozen official vehicles were parked bumper to bumper outside the Drexler mansion, some unmarked, others flashing police lights; curious neighbours leaned out of open windows, everybody asking questions. Kurt's mother returned, hauling plastic bags of shopping. When Colonel Stubbe of the MFS informed her about the nature of their visit, she almost fainted with shock.

'But the man was a former Jewish deportee. He told me he had been working in the Sonneberg mine where my father-in-law used to serve during the war.'

'That is possible,' Colonel Sedov, who could speak German well, interposed. 'He may have been a Hungarian deportee in the past, but now he is certainly an enemy agent. I am afraid we must question Herr Engineer Drexler.'

'Martin had no way of knowing that the visitor was an agent,' Helga Drexler protested. 'He only helped him during the war.'

At that remark Colonel Stubbe cut in somewhat impatiently, 'we would still like to question him personally. Herr Drexler must accompany us to the central station.'

'But he is so old and unwell . . .'

'He will receive the best medical attention. Kindly advise him to get ready.'

Her husband, Herbert, arrived, pale and shaken. Now close to crying, Helga told him what had happened.

Then she insisted on speaking again to Colonel Sedov, her voice now shrill with anxiety. 'My husband is absolutely innocent!'

Sedov listened patiently, but then made a quiet gesture over to Colonel Stubbe. 'Colonel Stubbe is in charge, Frau Drexler. I am only an observer.'

'I have been a loyal party member for fifteen years . . .'

'Frau Drexler, you have nothing to be concerned about.

We are ready to give you the benefit of the doubt,' Stubbe said. 'It was your own brave son, Kurt, who came forward with this important information.' He patted the boy on the head. 'You have done your duty for the party very well, young man, and you shall have your reward.'

'I did not do it for the reward, Comrade Colonel.'

'I am sure you did not.'

Frau Drexler went upstairs to help Martin Drexler get ready. Two Vopos guards followed her.

Turning back to Kurt once more, Colonel Sedov said, 'did you know that a boy just like you has had a statue erected in his honour in Kiev?'

Kurt nodded knowingly. 'I know . . . Oleg Kosevoi, whose parents collaborated with the Nazis during the occupation. After the liberation he denounced his renegade parents to the authorities and he was proclaimed a Hero of the Soviet Union.'

'Bravo,' Colonel Sedov complimented, smiling benevolently.

The soldiers who had gone upstairs with Kurt's mother returned, pushing Martin Drexler's wheelchair. Herbert rushed to aid his father, but the old man waved him aside. 'You stay out of this, Herbert. You have nothing to do with this affair which, I hope, will be resolved quickly.'

Nevertheless, Herbert wanted to accompany him to the station, but Colonel Stubbe declined his request.

'I am sorry, but that will not be possible. Don't worry. Herr Drexler will be well looked after.'

Helga gave her father-in-law another blanket to put over his knees. 'I am so sorry,' she sobbed quietly. 'But Kurt simply wasn't thinking,' she went on, trying to excuse her son.

The Vopos rolled the old man out and lifted him into a waiting army van, which drove off immediately.

From the ivy-clad terrace of the large, elegant hunting lodge, Harari used his binoculars to scan the surrounding woods and the rough dirt road which led down to the entrance to the coal mine. Jacques Moura's equipment had already been carefully removed from the Mercedes. They were ready to move on, but, after having looked again at the schedule of the border patrols, Harari wanted to get going straight on to the critical stage, when the risk of unwanted encounters would be minimal. According to his calculations, by 18.30 hours, the patrol should be back on the actual frontier-line, leaving the road completely unattended for about thirty minutes.

At 18.28 they all clambered back into the Mercedes and set off. The dirt road seemed negotiable and Harari wanted to save time and physical effort for the rigours of the mine.

The Mercedes rolled over the broken gate and turned into the road.

'Only two miles to the mine,' Cohen remarked.

'Batten down the hatches,' Jorv warned. 'We're in for some rough driving.'

Colonel Stubbe was content. It hadn't taken long to run the invalid engineer into contradictions, mistakes and retractions, and then screw the truth out of him, or at least the important part of it. The agents intended to escape through the demolished coal mine. Did they not know that the galleries were impassable? They had been blocked up years ago. Should they manage to get into the mine, they would be cornered in one of the blocked galleries like rabbits in a hole, with no exit.

He called for Captain Dieter Helms, who commanded the hundred-strong Dzerzhinski detachment, the DDR's crack security force, and ordered him to depart immediately for the Sonneberg mine.

'If you run into the enemy team while they are still in the open, arrest them. If they resist at all, gun them down, but try to capture Goldman alive.'

Then he went to see his Soviet counterpart.

Colonel Sedov did not interrupt Stubbe's enthusiastic scheme for cornering the agents inside the coal mine, but like his superior in Berlin, he too had had his reservations and was not inclined to underestimate the enemy. Professor Goldman was a Jew. The pseudo-Hungarian was a Jew, and very likely the others were too. 'I think we are up against an Israeli team,' he told Major Riumin, 'and the Israelis never undertake a project unprepared.' Major Riumin was in accord.

'Past Israeli achievements speak strongly against any such idea being a haphazard venture,' he said.

Speaking to Colonel Stubbe, Sedov asked warily, 'are you sure that the galleries which extend into West Germany are effectively blocked?'

Stubbe spread the floorplan of the mine on Sedov's desk. 'By your leave, Comrade Sedov . . .' and began to point out the number of collapsed sections and the extent of the damage to each of them.

'Twelve metres here . . . nine metres . . . ten metres,' he said forcefully. 'Nothing but fallen rocks and timber. Tons of it . . . Second level – three demolished sections. Rubble, rubble, rubble – each eight to ten metres long.' He stabbed at the map with his forefinger. 'How could anyone clear all that rock without heavy machinery? Without adequate manpower? Not five exhausted people, anyway. Two of them elderly and one a woman. Not in a million years, Colonel Sedov.'

'Remember that one of them is an expert,' Sedov reminded him. 'The Hungarian Jew worked in the mine for a long time.'

'That won't help them much. The Sonneberg mine is a compendium of disasters.'

But Colonel Sedov still had his misgivings, had the notion that something just didn't click. The fugitives most likely still possessed some as yet unplayed cards. He hoped, but could not believe, that Colonel Stubbe was right in his assessment of the situation.

He rose ponderously. 'Let's go to Sonneberg. On site, we may know better how things really are.'

9

'HORSESHIT!' AMRAN swore as the wheels hit a pothole with a terrific jolt that tossed everyone up to the roof. Harari, who had almost bitten off his tongue, called irritably, 'step on the brake, man, or else we'll fall down into the mine, car and all!'

Holding on to the door-brace, Professor Goldman grunted in discomfort while Darit and Ariel attempted to hold him steady. The Mercedes performed a slurring brake and the speed dropped, but even so the last stretch of the trip was a bumpy one. The wheels popped up and down in potholes, animal burrows and steep ridges.

'How much of a lead do we have?' the professor asked, gingerly rubbing his elbow which had been banged against the window.

Turning half-way round, Harari replied, 'perhaps half an hour.'

'Unless the commies send in helicopters to search us out,' Amran interposed dryly, then yelled, 'hold on!'

He twisted the steering wheel sharply, barely missing a five-foot-deep ditch filled with murky water.

'There it is.' Ariel Cohen spoke, pointing forward.

The car was heading towards a wooden barrier displaying the customary warning: '*Achtung! Grenzgebiet! Eintritt verboten.*'

Attention! Border Zone. Off Limits.

Instead of slowing down, Amran stepped on the

accelerator. The car smashed through the red and white striped beam and rolled on.

'Our poor Mercedes,' Darit complained quietly. 'I would have loved to take her back to Israel.'

'Me too,' Harari added. 'Ariel, how far must we go now?'

'Less than a mile, I think.'

STOP!

Another barrier. This time made of concrete. Amran cut the engine and stated flatly: 'The end of the line, fellows.' He scrambled out of the car, went to the trunk and shouldered the bazooka, the satchel containing the shells and dynamite and the Uzi machine gun. Harari and Cohen both took weapons, grenades, gas masks and the scuba gear. Professor Goldman and Darit shared the burden of the food and water supplies and the medical kit.

'Which way?' Harari asked Cohen, who waved a casual hand.

'Straight on for the time being. There should be a clearing further ahead where the barracks of the French and Belgian POWs used to be.'

'How far from there is the entrance to the mine itself?'

'About five hundred yards.'

Harari suggested that they move on, keeping close to the edge of the woods, taking an overgrown footpath. They walked in single file, with Jorv providing the rear guard.

They had not progressed very much before the approaching clatter of a helicopter sent them scurrying for cover. 'Five-blade MiG 24,' Jorv commented expertly, then, as the machine swerved into a tight turn and almost stopped above the trees, he added, 'they've found the car.'

'And will now radio through to the troops where to look for us,' Ariel concluded.

He was right. Within a few minutes the Sonneberg complex was transformed into a site of hectic activity. A veritable squadron of helicopters zoomed in, dropping low over the few available clearings, spilling Vopos and platoons of the crack Dzerzhinski Brigade – fortunately some way off target. Dusk was approaching and, pressed by the Russians, Colonel Stubbe of the MFS urged his soldiers to get a move on. The half-track command van containing KGB Colonel Ivan Sedov and his staff lumbered into sight. The STASI brought in a dozen trained dogs. Very soon the troops fanned out and began to move across the forest, guns at the ready. It seemed impossible that anyone could remain undetected in the restricted area.

Shepherding Professor Goldman, the Israeli team hurried on, keeping under the trees. The four hundred yards which separated them from the pursuers was not much of a distance, but the mine was near.

Moments later Harari found himself face-to-face with a Vopo corporal, about to fire.

It was touch and go. Harari and the corporal pulled their triggers at the same time, except that by some reflex the Israeli captain also flung himself flat on the ground. He winced as the powerful slugs tore past his head. The corporal stared at him with wide eyes, incredulous that something as dreadful as death could really happen to him; then he folded up to twitch a couple of times and die, vomiting blood. Two of the corporal's companions were stopped by Amran's Uzi. The Vopos dropped their weapons and raised their arms, their eyes hollow with fear and howling, 'Nicht schiessen! – don't shoot!'

'I'm sorry, buddies,' Jorv apologised with genuine chagrin. As much as he wanted to be lenient, he fired two rapid shots at their thighs; his adversaries screamed and dropped down into the grass like felled deer. Jorv added sadly, 'otherwise you would only have come after us again.'

But the short exchange had brought the relentless pursuers on to the right track. Dogs barked in the distance and were approaching rapidly; shots rang and bullets whizzed past them to thump into the trees. The Israelis stumbled on, with Darit and Cohen helping Goldman over the rough terrain. Suddenly Jorv disappeared from sight. Dodging shrubs and tree-stumps, Harari had no time to look for him.

'*Halt!*'

The coarse challenge was followed by a crisp overhead salvo from a large weapon. A lanky frontier guard with legs set apart and gun at the ready blocked their path. Darit uttered a faint cry. Harari caught her roughly by the arm.

'On your bellies!' the guard commanded, his face radiant with satisfaction. 'Arms and legs apart!'

The Israelis obeyed.

Keeping them covered, the soldier reached for the whistle he carried in his breast pocket and lifted it to his mouth.

It was his last act in the world of the living.

Amran materialised behind him like a shadow. His commando knife glinted and swung round in a short arc, cutting off all but a brief, choked, gurgling sound. Darit turned her face away. Professor Goldman gazed in frozen horror at the ghastly sight. Amran eased the dying soldier into the grass and hurled his weapon into the thorny thicket in disgust.

'Where the hell have you been?' Harari hissed as they jogged on.

'Making a small detour,' Amran gasped. 'When I was a kid, we used to play Cowboys and Indians in the Colorado hills. I spotted the guard before he moved into the open. You didn't.'

Even while they were running, Darit tried to comfort Goldman, who did his best to alleviate her concern. 'I can hold on,' he reassured her in Yiddish. 'You need not worry about me.'

Harari turned. 'Where is that bloody wheelhouse, Ariel?'

'Not more than a hundred and fifty yards now.'

Then, without warning, Jorv's Uzi spat fire and the runners stumbled to an abrupt halt. Behind them two Alsatians rolled in the grass, howling in pain, twisting in agony.

'Oh God, the poor dogs.' Darit's face twisted with sorrow.

'Keep going!' Amran commanded her. 'Those "poor dogs" would have torn you to pieces in two minutes.'

Clambering over a narrow stretch of ploughed land and traversing a fifty-foot clearing, they landed, exhausted, at the wall of the elevator house and took shelter just as a hail of slugs tore up the earth around them.

Wham . . .

Harari staggered back against the wall and sat there for a moment, stunned. He had seen the muzzle-flash and heard the shot, felt the hard knock on the right side of his chest. But no pain followed, no rapidly spreading darkness and the bottomless pit of death. He felt none of the vague images of dying he had envisioned many times in the past. He stared into four pairs of anxious eyes and heard Darit's cry, 'Hadar! Are you hurt?'

He shook his head and looked down at his body. Then he saw it. The bullet had slammed into the hard, gridded iron casing of one of the grenades strung from his shoulder holster. Had it hit just a millimetre or two higher, it would have demolished the safety catch and set it off.

He scrambled up. 'A near miss,' he told his companions, and saw their vast relief.

He had to act quickly. The security forces were closing in, although for the moment Amran and Cohen had managed to pin them down in the shrubbery across the clearing.

The massive padlock on the great iron door frustrated Hadar's efforts. '*La'azazel*,' he swore between his teeth. 'Karlim should have left the bloody thing open.' Only later did it occur to him that the elevator house was situated directly on the regular beat of the border guard, and a passing soldier could have spotted the irregularity.

A bullet whined past his ear and he ducked. Then he

remembered the old soldier's maxim: 'The one you can hear isn't going to hit you.' The bullet slammed into the sheet-iron of the door, denting it. A final vicious wrench pulled the padlock free.

Then the random shots turned into a shower of copper-plated lead, though it was already too dark for precise shooting. Harari zig-zagged to the partly ruined engine house where his companions had taken shelter. 'Pass me the stovepipe,' he hissed to Amran, who pushed the bazooka within reach. Shouldering it, Harari caught a glimpse of Cohen blazing away furiously at a dozen grey shapes who had broken cover and were darting towards a toolshed on the flank. Two of them spun around and dropped like rag dolls, a third staggered on for half a dozen paces, halted and fell to one knee, clutched at his abdomen and pitched into the grass face first.

A grenade exploded and Ariel vanished in a plume of dust filled with shards of bricks, shredded grass and smoke. Bracing himself against a derelict machine, Harari took aim and fired. The bazooka shell tore off the left door-wing and demolished a section of the wall.

His next concern was Cohen.

To his horror, he saw Darit crawling towards where Ariel had been standing before the blast, with bullets raking the ground around her. 'Darit, are you crazy? Stay down!' he cried. She rose to one elbow and waved a hand. 'God!' Harari gasped in exasperation. 'She's a sitting duck out there.'

The smoke dispersed and he spotted Cohen, embracing the earth but moving slowly to meet Darit. From his swift progress Harari could see that he was unhurt. A miracle.

Cohen pulled Darit behind a pile of logs and clutched at his eyes. They were full of grit and he was spitting earth. Harari gasped with relief and then lobbed two smoke canisters into the clearing. Amran followed up with three more, and after a few seconds the billowing smoke blotted out the bushes on the far side. 'Run to the wheelhouse!' he yelled, and with a couple of strides they reached the interior and relative safety. The winch was there, properly set up, as promised by Karlim. Firing at random into the rolling smoke, Amran followed them, pausing at the entrance to chuck two last grenades.

The smoke both covered their retreat and delayed the advance of the enemy. Sheltering behind the loose iron door, Harari opened fire to delay their pursuit.

'Help Goldman with the winch,' he shouted to Amran. 'Let Ariel go first. He knows the way.'

Another grenade exploded close to the entrance, swinging the door and showering Harari with earth and shattered rock. Splinters clanked off the iron and chipped the brickwork; the pressure of the compressed air from the blast around him stabbed into his ears. Cursing through his teeth, he let loose another short salvo, then busied himself with the dynamite. Working as fast as he could in the smoke and the dying light, he cut the fuses to different lengths, hoping that the subsequent explosions would keep the enemy at bay. Or at least delay them long enough for him to descend the shaft and get down to the first level.

Professor Goldman was already on his way down. With her knapsack strapped on, Darit waited for her turn. Jorv stood by to assist her.

They had not planned to enter the coal mine under gunfire, but so far everything was going well. They were all alive and unhurt, and already descending. Inside the mine, the enemy's numerical advantage would disappear. Only three or four of them could advance together in the narrow galleries.

Harari glanced at his watch. The others should already be down.

More troops darted across the clearing. Another short burst of the Uzi from Harari compelled them to drop and crawl.

Their descent proceeded smoothly. Ariel landed first and braced himself against the shaft framework. He waited for the professor, who lowered himself slowly, cautiously, with Jorv giving a helping hand. When he was almost level with the floor, Ariel grasped his hand and helped him down onto the platform. 'What a trip,' Goldman gasped, then added with a thin smile, 'still, it is better than running across minefields and climbing over barbed wire fences.'

Darit called from above and Ariel resumed his former position. She came sliding down slowly, grasping the cables with her gloved hands, in perfect control of her movements. After a few moments she sprang lightly into the gallery.

'How far down are we, Ariel?'

'Two hundred and thirty feet, Darit.'

'Whew!' She stared up the shaft. 'What about Hadar?' she asked Amran.

'He'll come down in a few minutes.'

Back up in the wheelhouse, Harari's attention was caught by another pair of Alsatians who charged out of the thinning smoke and came dashing towards him. He gunned them down before they reached the entrance.

There were now shouts and swift commands quite close, and he heard the rumbling sound of a heavy engine. The outline of a stubby armoured car silhouetted against the crimson skyline came into view. Its turret, armed with a short, mean-looking gun, turned slowly and the muzzle shortened with perspective. Harari did not feel like waiting until it vanished completely as the gun came to bear down on him.

Someone fired a Very Light.

He lit the fuses on the four sticks of dynamite and hurled them far into the clearing. The fuses had been set at twenty, thirty, fifty and eighty seconds. The subsequent explosions should keep the enemy away from the elevator house just long enough to enable him to reach the first level.

He swung his gun onto his back, grabbed the bagful of explosives and leaped onto the cable, sliding down out of control into the abyss for a few yards before he got control of his descent. He paused to struggle on his heavy gloves. Sheltered as he was, he felt a fair amount of pressure from the first two-inch shell from the gun on the armoured car as it slammed into the wheelhouse above him, almost knocking the air out of his lungs.

He let himself slide down the cable, heard the first dynamite explode, counted slowly and heard the second blast, the third one much duller and the last one barely audible. He saw lights flashing from down below. The rugged walls of the shaft flowed past his eyes.

He heard excited voices from overhead. Shouts, orders echoing in the hollow space. A powerful searchlight swept the shaft. A voice commanded, 'Stop that winch!'

'Get down here fast!' Harari heard Amran's call and felt a grasping hand on his arm. A sharp, metallic clang cut through the momentary silence. He swung himself into Amran's steadying hold just at the moment the severed cable coiled past the landing and crashed down into the abyss.

'Just in time,' he gasped. 'They've cut the cable.' He bent forward to ease his shoulders, which were now burning from the effort of the descent.

'So much the better,' Jorv said with a shrug. 'I wonder how they intend to follow us down here.'

A little recovered, Harari turned to Ariel Cohen. 'Ariel, from now on we're all yours,' and gave him a friendly slap.

Cohen's eyes lit up. He hitched his trousers and pointed. 'This is the way.'

'What are our chances?' Professor Goldman asked.

'Better than ever,' Harari replied cheerfully. 'Our pursuers are going to take at least a couple of hours to work out a way to get down here in force.'

'And after that?'

'Well, for one thing, they're going to find it awkward coming too close, Professor. The galleries are narrow so none of our bullets can possibly miss. Besides, we plan to blow up the passages behind us to give them a bit more work.'

From above came a harsh shout. 'Stay where you are, you fools! You don't have a chance. Don't you know that the mine is blocked?'

'Balls!' Jorv yelled flatly, and gathered up the equipment he was to carry.

'Let me carry something too,' Professor Goldman insisted.

'You must carry yourself, Professor,' Harari smiled at him briefly.

'Oh, I insist.'

'Well, then – if you insist, you can help me with this kit.' Darit offered him her medical kit, which was light enough.

Torchlights ablaze, they followed Ariel along the slightly sloping gallery that was still fitted out with the original mine rails and rusty coal cars. Water seeped through here and there between the mouldy planks and rafters. The air was stale and damp, though good enough to breathe, but it was getting warmer all the time. The going was relatively easy until they arrived at the first demolition which Adin Karlim had already partly opened, making a passage just wide enough to squeeze through. Once they had all passed it, Harari and Amran immediately blocked it up again as best they could, without resorting to dynamite. A short way beyond the barricade stood the toolshed where Karlim had left them their extra equipment.

They discarded their by now tattered KGB uniforms and changed into overalls, donning helmets and boots. Not for the first time, Harari wondered how the hell Karlim had managed to ferry down so much stuff, unless he had made several trips.

Of course, he had been able to do it at leisure. He had not been pursued by an army of security troops.

Neatly wrapped in heavy plastic were ten more grenades and two machine guns: a stubby, Czech-made Scorpion and a South African Viper, each complete with spare magazines. Hadar was curious about where Karlim had got hold of the Viper.

Both guns were handy weapons, like the Uzi; ideal for fighting in restricted places.

'You certainly have organised everything well,' the professor said admiringly.

'This is why Israel survives and wins her battles,' Amran responded. 'We never leave anything to chance.'

Goldman smiled serenely. 'Not even this mine?' he asked, his voice carrying mild challenge.

Harari turned to look at him. 'As you know, Professor, Ariel worked down here during the war. We also have a groundplan and a fair idea of what to expect on the lower levels. Indeed, very little has been left to chance.'

'I am confident of your success.'

'*Our* success, Professor,' Darit corrected him.

Following Cohen, they moved deeper and deeper into the mine, stepping over crashed balks and chunks of rock, sometimes wading in knee-deep pools of water, or sticky mire comprised of clay, earth and coal dust. Collapsed timbers lay singly or in clusters here and there. They arrived at the second toolshed with its padlock shot away and the door left ajar.

'It must have been Karlim,' Jorv commented, peering into the shed. Except for a few tattered and rusting helmets, lamps and picks, it was empty.

A few yards from the shed ran the second elevator shaft, the entrance of which was blocked with rubble. A large junction came next, where several galleries converged, strewn with a dozen battered coal cars. Unhesitatingly, Ariel chose the left-hand-side gallery. His certainty of the route lifted the spirits of his companions. Here, too, the ruined sections had been rendered passable by Adin Karlim, but Hadar and Jorv stopped after each obstacle to block it up again, with Cohen and Darit assisting in the work.

Jorv unpinned a grenade and wedged it carefully between a pile of massive fallen timbers. 'I'm leaving a "Good-night, Fritz" message for the STASI,' he explained with a grin. Carefully he arranged the trap. 'They move

162

just one of these balks and – boom! It'll make sure that the rest of the commies won't be going out of their way to catch up with us.'

'How far is it to the second level now?' Professor Goldman asked, tapping Cohen on the arm.

'Some three hundred yards down the slope. Another two hundred yards to the third toolshed, and one hundred more to the second elevator shaft, which is where we will have to descend again.'

'Without a winch this time?' asked Darit.

'The wall framework of that shaft is shaped almost like a ladder, and we can hold on to the cables,' Cohen answered reassuringly. 'There is no other way.'

'Then – that's it,' Amran commented.

10

Major General Pavel Podgorski was called by General Sherbakov over the direct line to the KGB headquarters in Moscow.

'Comrade Podgorski, where are we now in this matter?' he asked calmly. 'Do you yet have any idea where the agents came from? America, England, France, West Germany?'

Podgorski reported, even-voiced, 'I have reason to believe that we are dealing with Israelis, Comrade General.'

'*Bozhe moy!*' Sherbakov exclaimed, citing God; perhaps not in line with good communist practice, but in his position he could afford it. 'Now we have them on our backs too . . . Still, I am not surprised. Mossad's been spreading its wings lately, and Jakov Abramovich Goldman is Jewish. We made a mistake, allowing him to go to Berlin.'

Secretly rejoicing over his chief's dud, Podgorski responded in a tone of infinitely gentle reproval. 'I have always considered the Jews to be unreliable elements. They should not be permitted to occupy sensitive positions. Jews are too cosmopolitan, and it must be admitted that we have been in the habit of ignoring the Israelis, even though they are a shrewd, tough and hard-hitting lot. We should remember Eichmann, the Entebbe hijackers and the Arabs who hit the Israeli team at the Munich Olympics. They are all dead now. The Israelis hunted them down, one by one.'

General Sherbakov uttered a sound of bitter amusement

at his subaltern's hardly concealed lecture or, what was worse, reprimand.

'The team at work here is probably a crack outfit,' he grunted. 'Haven't you traced them yet!'

'Certainly I have, Comrade General. But there's a long trail of dead bodies behind them. They shot their way past the East German Dzerzhinski Brigade, killing six men and wounding nine.'

'What is the situation right now?'

'The fugitives are on the first level inside the coal mine, presumably in the top gallery, and moving along a slope which leads down to the second level with several demolished sections in between. Neither level two nor level three goes all the way through to the West German side.'

'Can they reach the lower levels? The ones that have exits on the far side of the frontier?'

'Not through the elevator shaft they used initially. It is totally blocked ninety metres down,' Podgorski answered expertly. The now much-thumbed groundplan of the mine was spread out on the desk in front of him.

A moment later he added, 'the Israelis must somehow get back to the second elevator shaft and descend down the cables.'

'A tough undertaking for Goldman, don't you think, Podgorski?'

'The agents are carrying special equipment, and explosives.'

'They must have had local helpers to set this up.'

'I am of the same opinion on account of the winch alone. It could not have been smuggled into the country in their car.'

'That Mercedes must have been a veritable warehouse of contraband.'

'Our experts are still examining it,' Podgorski replied. 'The registration number is being investigated in Paris. Perhaps Comrade Simonov will manage to trace the car to the garage where the bodywork was converted.'

'Let me know every new development, no matter how

small. If Simonov discovers the workshop, we might be able to eliminate an important Israeli base in France. Spare no effort or expense. Jakov Abramovich Goldman must be brought back to Moscow, or eliminated. He is carrying vital military secrets.'

'Not on his person, Comrade General, that we know for certain.'

'He is carrying everything in his head, Podgorski. Goldman's brain is like a sponge. It absorbs everything.'

Directing the operation from his command half-track armoured car, KGB Colonel Ivan Sedov was feeling exhausted and depressed. Things were not going easily, just as he had foreseen.

'Give me the latest progress report,' he ordered Colonel Stubbe of the East German STASI.

'Our technicians are about to restore the electricity supply to the mine,' came the sure-voiced reply. 'Then we will be able to use some of the elevators, pneumatic hammers and drills and other machinery to speed up the work. A group of miners are already on site, and a platoon is already in gallery one, in pursuit of the fugitives.'

'Speed it up, Comrade Stubbe. I recommend you – speed it up.'

'It is not easy, Comrade Sedov. As the agents advance, they are blowing up the gallery behind them. We have huge piles of rubble to clear, some of them as much as fifty feet long. It takes time to clear the way.'

'How much time?' Sedov asked impatiently.

'In some cases, hours!'

'The Israelis must be facing similar obstacles,' Colonel Sedov reflected. But, at that, Stubbe uttered a dismal laugh.

'Certainly, but they don't have to look for booby-traps. The bastards are not only demolishing the gallery, but they are also concealing primed grenades in the debris. Four of our soldiers have already been killed, and another six have had to be taken to hospital. Searching for bombs is a time-consuming business.'

'Any developments regarding their local contact?'

'We suspect a resident agent who has access to military supplies,' Colonel Stubbe replied. 'A section of MFS is working on that angle.'

There was a pause while Colonel Sedov studied the groundplan again. He glanced up. 'Is there no way to get ahead of them? Perhaps through one of the ventilation shafts?'

'They are only two feet wide, and most of them are blocked. Nevertheless, our engineers have already thought about the necessity of finding a short cut.'

'Could you explain this scheme to me in detail?' Sedov queried, tapping the groundplan.

'Certainly,' the STASI officer answered. 'This dotted red line shows the only route the agents can take in order to reach the West German side down on the sixth level. That's nearly three hundred metres below the surface.' He traced the converging galleries with his finger. 'The upper passages extending across the border have been too extensively damaged. No one could possibly negotiate them without using heavy machinery. Levels five and six do have connections, but both might well be flooded.'

Sedov cut in, 'if that is so, it should mark the end of this insane escape attempt.'

Colonel Stubbe shook his head and replied glumly. 'Unfortunately it's not that simple. There is a set of drainage valves on level five. They let the water drain into the very deepest, inactive galleries specially excavated for that purpose. We know that the Israelis have an expert guide with them. They are moving fast, invariably in the right direction, despite the fact that the mine is a genuine maze of tunnels.'

Colonel Sedov pursed his lips, tilted his head back and asked quietly, 'is there any possibility of getting gas down into the lower sections?'

'Gas?'

'Yes, tear gas – or something similar.'

Colonel Stubbe sent for one of the mining engineers who was familiar with the Sonneberg complex. The engineer listened to Sedov's proposal, then answered evasively.

'To do that, the ventilator rotors would have to be reversed. The work would take days.'

'We have only hours,' the KGB officer commented dryly. 'Perhaps not even that.'

The engineer waited patiently, but, as no further suggestion was forthcoming, he prompted, 'is there something else you wish me to do, Comrade General?'

'Yes. Help us to stop Goldman and the agents. Alert the entire neighbourhood. Bring in more pit workers. Use dynamite if necessary. Blow up the whole bloody mine. I don't care. Just stop the fugitives.'

'I understand your anxiety to get this job done, Comrade Sedov, but what we may or may not do depends on the MFS in Berlin . . .' Stubbe responded warily.

'On Lieutenant General Stutz – I know, but it is you who commands here, Comrade Stubbe. You are the man in charge of this operation.'

'General Stutz is my superior officer. He will resent it if I countermand his orders.'

Through clenched teeth Colonel Ivan Sedov murmured something about Stutz taking a trip to Vorkuta, but said aloud rather impatiently, 'get him on the phone, Comrade Stubbe. I'll talk to Stutz myself.'

With Ariel Cohen and Jorv Amran leading the way some twenty yards ahead, Harari, Darit and Professor Goldman advanced in what was perhaps the worst section so far. The passage was partially filled with large lumps of sodden coal, slimy, rotted timber struts and jagged boulders. Several times they blessed Adin Karlim's foresight for having provided rubber boots, which helped them wade through the frequent pools of disgusting slime that had collected over the years. Loose, broken rafters and planks, many of them splintered and as sharp as lances, constituted another danger. Ever aware of Goldman's heart condition, Harari allowed them all to take frequent breaks. Each time they stopped, Darit would ask after the professor's state of health, check his pulse, blood pressure, and administer the medicines he needed. She, too, had noticed that the elderly scientist was doing his utmost not to become a burden; he kept up with his younger companions to the best of his ability, without ever asking for a rest. Nevertheless, Goldman felt himself very much out of his element in the mine and, although he never showed any sign of slackening, sometimes his confidence ebbed.

When they all stopped to rest, the distant rumble caused by an army of working hands wielding picks and pneumatic hammers was clearly audible. The sounds of hectic activity in the distance never ceased, and occasional dull explosions indicated that the enemy too were blasting to make better headway. Their pursuers never seemed to stop for a rest. When one team became exhausted, another took its place.

It was already past midnight. They had been inside the mine for seven hours and were beginning to feel the strain. Clearing a way across the roof-high piles of debris, then blocking them up again without the proper tools, was excruciatingly hard work. Wisely, Jorv wanted to preserve the last remaining sticks of dynamite for emergencies. More than once he thought to himself that he would have preferred to go through three more Entebbe actions rather than across another fifty-foot stretch of Sonneberg. According to the groundplan from Martin Drexler, there were still seven more demolished areas to cross, and God only knew what the situation in the lower sections would be like. Without regular maintenance, some of the galleries and shafts could have collapsed, rocked by underground movements, eroded by ground water, or simply wrecked

169

by natural decay. Jorv felt like a submarine fighter living through a sustained depth-charge attack.

After a laborious advance of some four hundred yards, the team rested again. Darit opened a tin of corned beef and prepared rough though filling sandwiches for everyone. Meanwhile Amran boiled instant coffee over four glowing cubes of petroleum spirit. Along with Harari and Cohen, he had just finished clearing a passage across a twenty-foot pile of rubble which, as soon as they were through, had had to be blasted back into place. The sight of the massive pile of crushed wood and stone that barred the way of their enemies instilled a temporary sense of security in them. The way to the second elevator shaft by which they planned to reach the third level was free. However, they all desperately needed a rest before making the strenuous descent down the elevator cables. They would have to use improvised straphangings and short lengths of rope made secure with cleats. Ariel thought the cables should be free from grease after so many years of disuse, which would provide makeshift handholds. He was now quite eager to see the third level with its fourth toolshed. There stood the old Jewish quarters where he had lived and slaved for over seven months.

'All my respect to the miners,' Professor Goldman remarked, sipping his coffee, before questioning his companions further about life and customs in Israel, not wishing to arrive there like a greenhorn, lost in his new life. Naturally, the forever-present Palestinian question turned up, and the subject drew an instant sneer from Jorv. 'The "Palestinian Question" is being kept alive by malicious intent,' he snapped. Harari made a half-hearted effort to curb Amran's oncoming tirade, which he himself already knew by heart, but the volatile lieutenant continued unabated, perhaps just for the professor's benefit, and within moments he was submerged in this well-known theme.

'All the rich Arab nations loathe the idea of resolving the

Palestinian refugee problem,' he stated with conviction. 'They don't want any solution, except at Israel's expense. Or should we believe that the oil sheiks haven't got sufficient money to build ten-room villas for every refugee family? Or land enough to provide the Palestinians with a country twice as large as Israel? Balls!' he sneered. 'The sheiks are spending a hundred times as much on military hardware, Professor. They also buy luxury hotels in Europe, land in the States, shares in important industries. The wealthy Arabs prefer to keep their have-not brothers in shanty towns, deprived and desperate, because people with regular jobs, living in good homes and with children going to school, would no longer roam the streets with Kalashnikovs in their hands ready to kill or get killed . . . Two-thirds of Saudi Arabia is empty, including a lot of the shore-line, where the refugees could be settled to found a nation. And if they complain about the land being a desert, they should be told, "Look what the Israelis have done in the Negev. Get to work and do the same." But the Arabs don't want to labour. They only want to grab what is ready.'

'There is some truth in all this,' Harari conceded, taking over while Jorv paused to catch his breath. 'The Russians are even less eager to help us find a solution. Tranquillity in the Middle East would not serve their expansionist designs. Besides, weapons must be paid for in easily convertible currency. The Kremlim needs oil dollars to buy American wheat. And peace would not justify their armed presence in the Middle East, just as general world peace would not justify their presence anywhere outside the USSR.'

'The communists can fish only in turbulent waters,' Amran cut in. 'Their hunting grounds are the deserts of human misery. Where people are content, communism is as dead as a doornail.'

Professor Goldman asked mildly, 'is it not true that the Israelis confiscated the property of thousands of local Arabs; turned them out of the country like homeless vagrants?'

171

Jorv held up a restraining hand. 'Just a minute, Professor Goldman —'

'That is what they told us all the time in Russia,' the old scientist concluded.

'We can believe that,' Harari spoke before Jorv could open up again. 'We did indeed confiscate the property of our armed enemies and their helpers. Palestinians who had gone to fight alongside the Arab Legion, the Egyptians in the Ghaza, and the Syrians in the north. When they returned after the armistice, they did find their houses razed, or occupied by Jewish settlers.'

Jorv cut in impatiently, 'Should we have given them a reward for having tried to stab us in the back?'

Harari silenced him. 'Will you for once permit me to finish?'

'Go ahead.' Jorv sat back sullenly.

'There were many other Arabs whose property had been bought,' Hadar went on, addressing Goldman. 'Purchased for cash – hard currency. At the time the sellers rejoiced over their good deals. They even mocked the stupid Jews. The money was usually more than sufficient for them to settle in any other country and start new businesses. But the majority of the fellows went off to bust the cash in Beirut night-spots and gambling houses, on fancy women and in luxury shops. Then, when the money was gone, they moved into refugee camps to milk the UN and began hollering about having been robbed by the Zionists. Decent Arabs who shared in the labour with us, and who did not join our enemies in the hope of easy loot, are still at home, in Israel, pursuing their trades.'

'Are there any Arabs in the Israeli Defence Force?' Goldman asked.

'Some trusted civilian helpers, yes,' Harari replied. 'Not active servicemen.'

'Why not?'

'Mostly because the majority of Israeli Arabs have close relatives in the neighbouring countries and are open to influence by family sentiments, or to blackmail. It would be risky to integrate them into the armed forces.'

'Understandable,' Goldman agreed.

Jorv asked jestingly, 'and how's life in the USSR?'

Goldman smiled. 'Life in Russia is very tranquil, based on the principle of "what you don't know, you won't miss" – such as comfort and luxury, but principally freedom. The Russians are frugal people. They notice hardship less than others. To keep them in line, the party only needs policeman, grandiose parades and sports festivals. The individual has no existence, except as part of the state, and always subordinates himself to the requirements of the state.'

'Do the Russian people not recognise this?' Darit interposed for the first time. 'They really do not know anything else?'

Goldman retorted serenely, 'in the USSR the people do not need to know anything. They only need to believe, Darit.'

'How awful,' she said curtly.

Ariel, who had gone to examine the second shaft, returned with a grave look on his face.

'What's wrong?' asked Harari.

Ariel shrugged. 'Something doesn't tally here,' he announced, sitting down wearily on a boulder. 'The elevator cables should have been dry after all these years, but I found them slick with grease . . . new grease.'

'You think the elevator has been used recently?'

'That is the only explanation, Hadar.'

The two men exchanged glances. They had both grasped the ominous significance of Ariel's discovery. Perhaps the STASI had found a way to get ahead of them.

Beckoning Jorv to come along, Harari followed Cohen to the shaft. Shading their flashlights, the two officers examined the cables.

'There's no doubt,' Jorv said. 'The elevator has been used in the last few weeks.'

173

'We saw the shaft blocked on the first level.'

'The STASI could have cleared the debris, brought in electricity, and got down to level three the easy way.'

'But not so easy for us,' Harari commented grimly.

'The carriage is still down,' Ariel reminded them.

'Which can only mean that somebody's trying to set a trap,' said Jorv.

'Silence!' Hadar spoke in a subdued voice.

They heard a sharp, metallic clang. Then the cables moved.

'The carriage is coming up,' said Ariel.

'Probably to ferry down more troops,' Harari remarked. 'How many men can the carriage take, Ariel?'

'This one, only five or six. But the principal elevator could easily fit in twenty.'

Jorv Amran unpinned a grenade. 'Let's cut off their reinforcements,' he said with a grin. When the elevator carriage arrived, he placed the grenade on top of it.

'Now run for dear life!'

The three men bolted back up the gallery, the dull boom of the blast and the sounds of cascading metal and stone following them all the way.

Harari briefed Darit and Goldman on the new development, then turned back to the groundplan.

'There's only one way to turn the tables on them,' Jorv said after a while. 'Two of us must descend the number fifteen ventilation shaft, which, according to this, is free of debris. Then we must get behind the buggers through the old Jewish workers' quarters.'

'That shaft is only twenty-five inches wide,' Ariel reminded him.

'That should just about be enough, if we don't take our rucksacks,' Jorv countered. 'The nylon rope is long enough.'

'Yes, we've one hundred feet of it,' added Harari.

'But they might hear you coming,' Darit said in a voice tight with anxiety.

'The shaft is at least seventy feet from where the soldiers

are probably waiting,' Hadar answered reassuringly. 'I'm going down with Jorv. You and the professor will wait for our call, then make your descent. The framework is almost like a ladder, with horizontal girders at five-foot intervals.'

He left with Amran, carrying only pistols, grenades and the coil of rope, watched by Darit's worried eyes. The shaft was not quite as wide as a street manhole, but to their pleasant surprise it was made of tin tubing, so the two men were able to escape the discomfort of bruising themselves against jagged rocks and veins of coal. Having fastened the rope to a pair of tough timbers, Jorv entered first, with Hadar following some yards behind. Carefully, the two descended, gripping the rope with heavy leather gloves, checking their rate of descent by bracing against the sides of the tube. They made as little noise as possible, and did without the benefit of their flashlights. Minutes passed. Ten? Twelve? Fifteen? They could not tell in the pitch dark. Suddenly Jorv felt a strong draught, the tube widened and his back lost contact with the sides. He swung free, still descending. After a few heartstopping moments his feet touched the ground, and an instant later Hadar joined him.

For a while they stood, frozen, listening, but the silence was absolute. Shading his battery torch with one palm, Harari surveyed the place. They were standing in a twenty by sixty foot excavated cavern, with the ventilation shaft overhead, rising up over two rows of three-storey wooden bunks and a few roughly-nailed tables; everything covered with dust, rotted away, holed by worms, chewed by rats. Most of the furniture was collapsed, broken or askew. The air was warm and damp. 'This is probably where Ariel slaved,' Harari whispered.

Bolted to the roughly-hewn wall a decayed plank still carried the faded Nazi slogan lettered in bold Gothic characters: '*ARBEIT MACHT FREI*' – work makes you free. A nameless inmate, probably long dead, had written over the words, '*Nur Tod*' – only death. And there were names still discernible, hundreds of them, and what could

175

have been farewell messages, carved pathetically into every flat slab of stone. The aura of death and suffering seemed to have sunk deep into the very walls.

'Let's move on,' Jorv suggested in a subdued voice.

Their rubber-soled boots made no noise. Using the fingers of one hand stretched forward to detect obstacles ahead of them, the Israelis advanced carefully, managing to avoid a pair of fallen timber struts and an overturned coal car. Counting his paces, Harari estimated the distance they had already covered. At length he halted, drew close to Jorv and whispered, 'I think there are only a few yards to go. Get ready.'

In the darkness someone cleared his throat. It sounded close, damn close. Harari drew his automatic and Jorv unpinned a hand grenade.

'Now!'

The grenade rolled into the gallery and immediately the two took shelter behind the abandoned coal car. The blast was tremendous. It illuminated the tunnel as lightning lights up the sky. They saw the shapes of men as they were flung in every direction; savage yells and screams of anguish stabbed into their ears. Turning on their torches, the two Israelis charged forward, blazing away at anything that still moved in the smoke-filled gallery.

Surprise had been absolute. There was no return fire. Jorv's grenade seemed to have landed right on the waiting group of security troops and peppered them with splinters, crushed them under collapsed timber and boulders.

'We got them all,' Jorv remarked coolly. 'I'm going to call the others.'

A quarter of an hour later they were together again. To Harari's surprise Ariel no longer wanted to visit his one-time living quarters. 'We shouldn't waste time,' he said, declining Harari's offer to take a short break. There were more barricades to clear, and to raise up again. In any case, that particular place had no special significance. Ariel Cohen had been here, there and everywhere. Every yard of the accursed place reminded him of some miserable

176

event. He led them along another slope which led down to the fourth level. There it ended at a short elevator shaft down to level five.

During a brief stop, Jorv asked warily, 'are there any more places where the STASI can get ahead of us?'

Ariel shook his head. 'Not unless they drill a new shaft through the rock, Jorv. By the time they finish drilling we should be safely back home in Israel.'

'*Inshallah*,' Jorv commented in Arabic.

Goldman asked, speaking in Yiddish to Amran, 'have you done many similar jobs in the past?'

'Some —'

'And were you never scared?'

'Of course I was scared,' Amran responded almost indignantly. 'I have had to change my underwear a few times . . .'

The professor uttered a soft laugh. 'Are you worried now?'

'My dear Professor,' Jorv said. 'For the moment, I'm pretty booked up on worries. I can't possibly start worrying about anything else for at least five days.'

'By then we'll be in Tel-Aviv,' Darit joked.

11

EXHAUSTED, NOW black with mud and coal dust, the small team at last reached the crucial stage of their subterranean quest – the elevator shaft to level five that provided the only method of descent. Having sat Professor Goldman and Darit in the comfortably dry toolshed near the shaft, Harari, Jorv and Ariel went to take a look and see if the way was free, and to take stock of the situation. But not even the powerful beams of Hadar's heavy-duty torch could reach the bottom of the dark pit. 'Abandon hope, all ye who enter here.' Amran cited Dante. Harari was convinced that he could see water glinting down below – not an uplifting thought. Grabbing a lump of coal, he dropped it down the shaft, counting the seconds as it fell. The splash came from a depth of about two hundred feet. Level five was flooded, perhaps also level six – their only way out to the Western side of the frontier.

This eventuality had been foreseen, but, even so, the fact of it was depressing. Although Amran had blasted the slope behind them in three separate places, the resulting obstacles might not hold back their pursuers long enough for him to dive into the flooded gallery, open the drainage valves – assuming that they could be opened – and then ascend again. Even with the valves open, it would be some time before the gallery drained sufficiently to enable them to continue.

Deep in thought, the three returned to the toolshed to find the professor reclining against the wall, taking a nap.

'Happy man,' Jorv remarked wryly, knowing that it was his job to dive into the watery abyss to try and open the valves. Not even Ariel could foretell the actual state of the gallery that was now filled to the brim with lukewarm water. For how long had those wooden planks that held up the ceiling been under water? Five years? Ten years? Wood deteriorates swiftly in tepid water. Would the ceiling hold? There was only one certainty: that they could not give up and turn back.

'What if level six is flooded as well?' Jorv asked Ariel gravely.

But Cohen shook his head vigorously. 'No, no – level six has open outlets into the lower sections. If you manage to open the valves the water will cascade all the way down to level nine.'

Amran was not wholly convinced. 'All the lower sections might be filled already, Ariel,' he argued. 'The mine has not been surveyed for twenty years.'

But Ariel's response sounded determined. 'Level nine has natural outlets, Jorv.'

Harari cut in, 'Where to?' He wondered where the hell all that water could possibly flow when they were already so deep underground.

'Who knows?' Ariel shrugged. 'There must be an underground reservoir . . . A lake, perhaps, or some current. No water has ever accumulated in level nine.'

'Well, let's hope you're right,' Jorv commented, and tapped the scuba gear he had been hauling ever since they entered into the mine. 'At least I didn't lug this baby all this way for nothing.'

Darit wanted to prepare more snacks, but Harari urged her not to. 'Try to get some rest.' He stroked her hair for a moment.

'I am not tired.'

'Yes you are. We all are.'

She had been marvellous, he thought to himself. She never asked for a break, never complained, but took the hardship like himself. Likewise Professor Goldman, who

179

had been doing his best not to hinder or delay the flight, although it must have been very hard on him. Even Harari's well-trained and conditioned muscles ached all over. Their hectic evasion of the STASI onslaught had not been part of the calculations in the overall plan. Originally the Israelis had hoped to traverse the mine at leisure, without having the additional problem of an unending supply of armed men behind them in close pursuit. They were going to spread the journey over a couple of days. Now the whole thing had to be performed at breakneck speed.

Up on the slope, the enemy continued to work doggedly on the obstacles. The dull echoes of their pneumatic hammers and drills were suddenly drowned in a muffled explosion, followed by cries, then utter silence.

Amran's chin lifted and his mouth widened in a gleeful grin. 'That was one of my grenades going up,' he stated in matter-of-fact tones. 'Saying goodnight to the STASI Fritzes.'

Besmirched with powdered coal, his uniform in tatters, Captain Dieter Helms of the Dzerzhinski detachment of State Security stumbled into the junction where KGB Colonel Sedov and Major Riumin had set up their temporary command post.

'Another of their damned grenades,' he complained, panting and spitting grit. Smoke and dust rolled after him, while from the gallery came cries of pain, bitter lamentations and filthy oaths. The Russians covered their faces with handkerchiefs. Major Riumin coughed. A small group of miners staggered out of the dark turbulence. They were covered in cuts and bruises, coughing, wiping their blood-shot eyes.

And hauling two corpses.

'*Sie machen uns zur Sau,*' Franz Pohl, their foreman, complained. He addressed the STASI captain and, casting a glance of dismay towards the Russians, added, 'they are slaughtering us.'

'Are there any more dead?' the captain asked, a miserable expression on his face.

'One more, but Engineer Strouha will probably die before we'll be able to get him out.'

'Where is he?'

'Under a ton of rubble,' Pohl replied gruffly. 'Yes, comrades – and you will have the glorious task of telling their wives and children. Sepp Mayer had three kids. Hans Ross two . . .' Without waiting for a response from the STASI captain, he beckoned his companions to move on over to the improvised first-aid station on the first level.

'Haven't you been using the detectors?' Colonel Sedov asked grimly.

Captain Helms uttered a bitter snort.

'Detectors are no use here, Comrade Colonel,' he answered. 'The galleries are full of iron. There are segments of railway, ten-inch nails and clamps in the balks, broken drillheads and bits of tools. They beep all over the place.'

There was a brief silence, then Colonel Sedov said gravely, 'the work must continue.'

Captain Helms would have liked to ask why the bloody hell the Soviet comrades could not have brought in their own troops and miners. But, of course, he held his tongue.

Five soldiers stumbled out of the gallery, rubbing their eyes and gasping for air. Their grim-faced sergeant made his report.

'The platoon has lost three more men.'

'Where are they?' asked Helms.

'Under the fallen timber.'

'You must get them out.'

'Let's get some breathable air in there first, Captain.'

Major Riumin interposed, 'where are the fugitives now?' He spoke directly to the sergeant.

'Some four hundred yards ahead of us, Comrade Major.'

'That is not much.'

'It's more than enough in those narrow, *gottverdammte* galleries,' the sergeant responded with a hint of contemptuous anger in his voice. 'We have two more demolished sections to clear, perhaps booby-trapped with more grenades.'

'How long will it take to clear those two sections?' Colonel Sedov asked meditatively.

'At least two hours,' replied the sergeant. 'But that isn't really the problem, Comrade Colonel. By the time we clear them, the Israelis will have blasted two more sections.' Then he added sourly, 'perhaps the time has come to give up this chase.'

The STASI sergeant's sullen, perceptibly defiant tone made the KGB officers frown, and induced Captain Helms to interpose quickly in an attempt to head off whatever Sedov might want to say.

'Our best chance will be at level five which, according to the engineers, is almost certainly under water.'

Using the restored elevator, Major Riumin returned to the surface to transmit the scheduled report to General Sherbakov in Moscow.

Colonel Sedov wanted to stay close to the scene of action.

While Amran undressed down to just his overalls and scuba gear, he talked to Ariel Cohen about the drainage valves.

'They are fixed into the floor at fifty-yard intervals,' Ariel explained. 'Round steel doors with wheel-lock mechanisms, very much like a submarine's escape hatch.'

Happy to be of use, he explained to Jorv how the valves worked and warned him against trying to open them too wide. He could be sucked in by the resultant vortex.

'I'll keep that in mind,' Jorv reassured him.

'What if the wheels are rusted solid?' asked Professor Goldman.

'I'll have to blast them open,' Amran replied.

'It would be rather risky,' Ariel reminded him. 'The timers only last up to fifteen minutes.'

'I know,' said Jorv, then bent down to test his scuba equipment. 'If I don't make it back in time, I'll become a small part of Israeli history,' he added ironically.

'Don't be foolish, Jorv,' Darit reproved. 'If you blow yourself up, you'll blow us up, too. Take care, for heaven's sake.'

'Don't you worry, Darit. Jorv Amran has always taken good care of his own skin,' Jorv quipped. Then, turning to Ariel, he asked, 'what do you reckon? How long should it take for the gallery to drain?'

Ariel considered this for a moment before answering.

'It depends on how many valves you manage to open, and to what extent. Let's say a single valve, opened fifteen inches . . .' Ariel rubbed his chin. 'I should say, in about two hours' time.'

'That's too long,' Harari commented glumly. 'The Vopos will get the passage clear in less than two hours. I may have to blast one more obstacle in their way.'

Jorv said with gravity, 'go easy on the explosives, Hadar. We only have four grenades and two sticks of dynamite left, and we'll probably need those in gallery six.'

'Okay, I'll only use one of each.'

'I suggest you position the dynamite so that you need not blow it up unless absolutely necessary,' said Jorv. 'Otherwise, recover it.'

'I'll do that.'

'Well, then – I'm ready.'

His companions escorted him to the shaft. Professor Goldman suggested that he should carry a lifeline fastened to his belt, but Amran overruled the idea, saying it could get entangled in the rubble. He put on his heavy gloves and swung onto the cable. 'Hold the fort while I'm away,' he told Harari and Cohen.

'Good luck, Jorv.'

Keeping their torch-beams directed straight down, Hadar and Ariel illuminated Jorv's way.

He let himself slip down slowly, measuring the cable

183

between his clutched thighs, sometimes bracing his feet against the horizontal girders.

'How's it going?' Harari called from above. His voice reverberated in the narrow pit.

'Great so far,' Jorv yelled back. 'Keep the lights on me.'

At about sixty feet down, he paused to rest. He could see the water some thirty feet below him. The black surface was littered with floating debris, mostly bits of wood. After a couple of minutes he resumed his wary descent.

Just above the surface he stopped again, tested the air inlet on his mask, then let himself sink down into the water, pushing aside the floating obstacles. He submerged and turned on the waterproof battery torch. To his surprise the water was quite clear. He could see clearly the jagged walls, the elevator cables and rails. Flipping over, he continued, head first, pulling himself by the cables, then floated into the gallery. Mercifully it appeared to be intact. Leaving one of his two torches beam-up under the shaft to orient himself, he swam deeper into the gallery, trying to keep to the centre of the passage in order not to graze his air tank against the rough ceiling, or stir up the bottom sediment, thus obscuring his view. The massive ceiling struts still supported the roof, and the side planks were still there, God only knew after how many years. Not for the first time, Amran had to admire the thoroughness of German engineering. Obviously there had been no blasting on the fifth level.

Swimming forward with slow, careful strokes, he spotted the first valve, or rather the top of the wheel-lock that emerged from the mire on the shaft floor, a mixture of earth and pulverised coal. It did indeed look like a submarine escape hatch. Bracing his feet against two vertical balks, Jorv grasped the wheel and, with some effort, managed to wrench it open about ten inches before the escaping gigantic air bubbles hurled him against the ceiling as the water cascaded down into the lower levels. Rolling and buffeted by the sudden disturbance, fighting against the strong downdraught, he manoeuvred himself back into position and opened the valve a little further. Around him the gallery seemed to boil with swirling bubbles. The rising sediment obscured his view. The bubbles raced towards the elevator shaft and Jorv had to use all his strength to avoid being swept away. He was tossed against a floating log and hurt his left shoulder; the vortex tugged at his feet and the light of his torch dimmed, but just avoided being suffocated by the swirling darkness that rose from the bottom. Chunks of plank careered past him, and for a while he could do nothing but take shelter, keeping his face against the wall.

One hundred and twenty feet overhead, Harari and Cohen heard the rumbling sound of the bursting bubbles. 'Jorv has managed to open the valves!' Ariel exulted. 'There must be air in the lower sections!'

Darit and Professor Goldman joined in the rejoicing.

'We've almost made it, Professor,' Harari said cheerfully. 'There's only one barrier in gallery six, then a single-layer brick wall and, beyond that, West Germany.'

Down below, Jorv moved his torch close to his wrist-watch. He had been under water for eighteen minutes. His air reserves would last another twenty minutes. He did not dare to open the valve further because the turbulence and the downcurrent would have been too strong. He decided to try the next valve, fifty yards down the gallery.

Partly swimming, partly hauling himself forward by grabbing hold of the roof timbers, he moved on with difficulty, but after some twenty yards the water became clearer and he could see ahead. He swam straight into a pile of rubble where the gallery had partly collapsed, probably through decay. Cursing to himself over the waste of time, he surveyed the obstacle and found a break just wide enough to squeeze through, hoping that no more rubble would crash down while he was on the far side.

Here he encountered large floating timbers rocked by the current. Occasionally the great blocks of wood rushed headlong into the planks along the sides, thudding like battering rams. Any of them could have crushed him to death.

Sixteen minutes left.

He found the wheel of the second valve badly bent by a huge lump of rock that crashed down on it, making it impossible to open the hatch. Holding the torch between his knees and working with fingers made clumsy by his heavy gloves, he positioned the plastic charge, rolled a boulder over it for better pressure and put the timer on its maximum setting.

Fifteen minutes.

Within a quarter of an hour he had to be out of the water and back up the shaft. If he didn't make it, he would indeed become 'a small part of Israeli history'.

The others were all gathered at the top of the elevator shaft, waiting in tense expectation, while behind them in the blocked passage the Vopos were working furiously to open the way.

'How long is gallery five?' Harari asked tersely.

'The flooded section is about eight hundred yards long,' Ariel said.

Professor Goldman made a quick mental calculation. 'There must be about six thousand to seven thousand cubic yards of water inside the gallery,' he intoned knowingly. 'If the valves Jorv has opened drain at ten cubic yards per second, the level should be dry in about forty minutes.'

'Still too much time,' Harari said, looking grave. 'By then the STASI will be over on our side of the last demolition.'

Grabbing a Scorpion and the depleted bag of explosives, he bolted up the slope of the passage to where he wanted to blast. He positioned a single stick of dynamite with a five-foot fuse. The last barricade was only thirty yards from where he was working, and the sounds of men and machines were close. Harari could hear intense voices, grunting with effort, interspersed with the occasional barked command.

Suddenly he heard a sharp crack and saw a six-foot timber sway and crash down, leaving a ten-inch opening in the rubble from which an automatic weapon immediately began to blaze away. Instinctively, he threw himself behind a derelict coal car and fired back at random, but the enemy gun had him pinned down. Swearing between clenched teeth, he lit the fuse, then began to crawl backwards, hoping he would be far enough away when the dynamite went off. By good luck the STASI gunner too had spotted the rapidly diminishing fuse, for he abruptly ceased firing and shouted a warning. Instantly the work on the obstacle stopped. Harari clambered to his feet and raced back to the shaft. Behind him the gallery exploded and crashed down.

'We've gained another twenty minutes,' he stated, panting.

'Jorv is coming up!' Cohen called excitedly.

Harari rushed over to the pit. 'Jorv!' Are you okay?'

'Still alive and in one piece.'

'Stay where you are and relax for a minute. How much water is still left in the gallery?'

'About five foot – receding quickly. The elevator shaft is already dry.'

'All right, we're coming down.'

Having lost two further companions to Jorv's booby trap, the civilian miners refused to go on with the work.

'We're not in the bloody army, so we can't just be ordered to die for nothing,' their defiant foreman told Colonel Stubbe and Captain Dieter Helms.

'For nothing?' the colonel exclaimed, acutely annoyed. 'The fugitives are dangerous Zionist agents who must be captured or eliminated,' he argued. Then he fell silent. Of course, he could not compel the miners to go on working, nor could he summarily arrest them. The days of absolute power were over, even for the STASI. The period of *Nacht und Nebel*, 'Night and Fog' – a heritage of the Gestapo regime which used to carry people off to disappear into nothing – were gone.

The foreman only shrugged, unimpressed. 'Your Zionists are just about to leave the DDR,' he replied sarcastically. 'Therefore they can no longer be dangerous . . . Besides, it's about time we left the Jews alone for a change.'

'This has nothing to do with their being Jews,' Colonel Stubbe snapped. 'You are working for the good of our country and as party members —' he added, using patriotic sentiments as a last resort.

'*Ach*,' the foreman waved aside the coming well-known tirade. 'It's the Russians who want to get their mits on this lot, not the DDR.'

'It is one and the same thing.'

At that the foreman uttered a sound of digust. 'If it is one and the same thing, Colonel Stubbe, let our Russian comrades fly in their own miners,' he retorted. 'We are going home.'

He waved a beckoning hand and strode off. Chucking down their spades and picks, the sullen-faced miners followed him. The STASI officers made no effort to stop them.

Just then Colonel Ivan Sedov arrived with Major Riumin and two other officers. They stepped aside to let the miners through but, just as the weary men filed past him, Colonel Stubbe heard one of them mumbling, '*Die Russen konnen uns am Arsch lecken*' – 'The Russians can kiss our asses.'

Stubbe gave the gist of the situation to the Russians, including the pit workers' decision to quit. Sedov's only comment was a sardonic, 'are they allowed to do that?' But his astonishment seemed genuine. In the USSR, behaviour like that would be called sabotage, illegal striking, thus anti-state activity. But when he said this to Stubbe, the East German colonel responded with a sneer.

'Unfortunately, we are not in the USSR, Comrade Colonel.' Whether he meant it positively or negatively, Colonel Sedov did not know, but Stubbe's statement sounded so insincere that the Russian had to fight down a fit of laughter.

Then he saw the line of recovered corpses, among them a Russian drilling expert from Krasnodar, and he lost his inclination to laugh.

Goldman and the Israelis were still on the slope that led to level six. Now so close to deliverance, they discarded all unnecessary gear and ran, slipping and slithering on the muddy floor, clutching hands and supporting one another. They stumbled over obstacles, splashed sticky lumps of mire left and right and even managed to laugh at the awkwardness of the others.

'You look like a chimney sweep,' Harari teased Darit. She smiled and replied in the same spirit: 'You should see yourself.'

They were in high spirits for the first time since they had entered into the mine over eighteen hours before.

Jorv said it was 8.30 in the morning on the surface, then added wistfully, 'the first thing I'm going to do is have a bath, then I'll eat a king-size T-bone steak, then I'll sleep for an eternity.'

He wanted to use the rest of the dynamite to bring down one more load of wood, stone and coal. Harari thought it a good idea, so the two men got down to work in a narrow section where the timbers looked very worn and were already sagging perilously.

After the explosion Harari asked Cohen, 'how far down is level six?'

'Along the slope – some six hundred yards.'

'A long walk,' Jorv commented and tapped the side of a coal car. 'How about rolling down to save our breath?'

Harari caught Darit by the hips and lifted her into the car, climbed aboard himself and gave a hand to the professor. Cohen went next and Amran took his place at the back. 'Here we go.'

He loosened the brake and the car began to roll down

the slope, quickly gathering speed. 'Brake, Jorv,' Harari cautioned his friend. 'We might run into a minefall head first.'

But the car arrived at level six safely. The gallery seemed free of debris, although it was oppressively warm and soggy, and at intervals the floor was covered with large pools of water.

'Four hundred yards to the brick wall, and then, beyond it, freedom,' Harari uttered with reverence.

Passing under an air shaft, Ariel recoiled and halted.

'Shh – quiet,' he silenced his companions, who stared at him questioningly. Leaning closer to the bottom of the shaft, Ariel tilted his head and listened. The others heard it too; a soft rasping sound, barely perceptible clanking.

'They are trying to get down the shaft again,' Harari said in a subdued voice. He turned and ordered Darit and Goldman to move on.

He listened.

The KGB and the STASI were probably desperate by now, he reasoned, and ready to accept any risk.

Jorv shrugged and said coolly, 'why worry? Only one at a time can come down the shaft and the first ones will descend rather faster than they bargained for.'

Snapping home a fresh magazine, he fired vertically into the narrow shaft, playing the muzzle around in a tight circle.

A hollow-sounding desperate scream rolled down to them. Two Vopos in commando uniforms dropped down onto the sodden floor, their uniforms shredded and bodies ripped apart by the slugs. The first one was dead when he hit the ground. His companion's legs and arms were lacerated. Doubled up, he rolled in the mire, moaning in pain. Jorv tossed their guns into the shaft. Harari was ready to move on but Darit squatted down beside the wounded trooper and opened her first-aid kit. Fiercely Jorv grabbed her arm and yelled, 'there's no time for such humanities, Darit!' and pulled her away. They broke into a jogging run.

'What's wrong,' Harari gasped, then the darkness behind them exploded and the pressure of air made them stagger.

'Do you see now why we didn't have time?' Amran looked at Darit. 'The STASI are dropping grenades and their wounded comrade must have got the blast right between the eyes.'

'The gallery is open, Colonel Sedov. We can resume the pursuit. This time there are no booby-traps,' Captain Dieter Helms reported boisterously.

'The Israelis have run out of dynamite,' Sedov stated with contentment.

A Red Army sergeant arrived, hauling a field telephone, with two soldiers running behind him uncoiling the wires that linked it to the command van. There was a call for Colonel Sedov from Sherbakov. 'General Podgorski is on his way there,' Sherbakov rasped in his habitual crisp style. 'He is going to take charge of this operation in person.'

'Comrade General, we are about to conclude it,' Colonel Sedov reported, his vanity hurt. He did not believe that the KGB chief from Berlin could do the job any better.

There was a lengthy silence, which Sherbakov broke.

'Where are you now, Colonel Sedov?'

'We're on our way to level six, where the Israelis and Goldman plan to cross into West Germany. We are past their obstacles and will probably catch them up in a few minutes. The troops are already nearly there.'

Another pause, then Sherbakov spoke reprovingly. 'I was informed that level five is under water. Wasn't that the place where you were going to arrest the fugitives?'

Sedov tried to play for time. 'Unfortunately, their guide knew about the drainage vents, and even managed to open two of them, Comrade General.'

'How?'

'We found their discarded scuba equipment.'

'I see . . . They really were prepared for all eventualities, eh?'

'We will take them at the brick wall.' But immediately he added with less enthusiasm, 'unless they have already crossed into West Germany.'

'What do you mean, *unless*?' General Sherbakov barked irritably. 'I hope a deserted border isn't going to stop your men?'

Colonel Sedov swallowed the lump in his throat. 'Are you ordering us to continue the pursuit on the West German side, Comrade General?'

'Right up to the surface if necessary,' the Moscow official snapped. 'This action has been authorised by Comrade Andropov and the MFS in Berlin has been advised. There are no Bundeswehr troops inside the mine and there should be no obstacles, either. Go ahead with the pursuit. *Bring Goldman back to Moscow.*'

Just then Major General Podgorski arrived with his adjutants. He immediately took over the call from Moscow. Sherbakov repeated his order, but Podgorski had also had misgivings about the intrusion across the frontier.

'Comrade Sherbakov,' he argued, 'it is very likely that Professor Goldman and his escort shall be met on the far side of the wall, either by representatives of the Bundeswehr or by the Americans. Even then the Israelis —'

'Then gun them down!' Sherbakov yelled, cutting through Podgorski's protests. 'You have a free hand to do whatever is necessary. Dead witnesses don't talk. At worst, Bonn will send us a protest note – written, I hope, on soft paper. We will load the whole affair on to West German smugglers or the CIA. Get moving, Comrade Podgorski!'

Major General Podgorski shrugged and put the receiver back gently on its rest. 'There's nothing we can do but obey and hope for the best. Sherbakov's orders have been issued by Andropov. It has the seal of the Politburo.'

The Israelis came to a halt some twenty yards from the brick wall. The access was blocked with coils of barbed wire stretching from floor to ceiling. Upon the wall itself a

192

much faded warning: *STAATSGRENZE* – State Frontier.

'German exactitude,' Ariel commented wryly. 'Even a thousand feet below the surface in an abandoned mine, they put up a warning.'

Jorv had already gone to work. He tied a length of rope to the handle of his pick, threw it up onto the mass of coils and began to drag them down. Harari and Cohen gave him a hand, and within a few minutes the way to the wall was free.

Like a bolt of lightning out of the clear sky a burst of ammo from a machine gun erupted from the darkness. Bullets bit into the timber all around them, and ricocheted off stones and iron clamps close to Darit, who hurled herself aside. She was unhurt, but badly shaken. Harari swore aloud as a slug ripped along his forearm, drawing blood. 'Turn off the lights!' He shouted a desperate warning and pushed Professor Goldman into a narrow crack in the wall. 'Darit!'

'I'm all right,' she responded in a faltering voice from the darkness. Higher up in the gallery Amran was firing furiously, while sparks from the lighted fuse on the last stick of dynamite sizzled past his feet, rushing into the distant gloom. The pursuers stopped firing and fled higher up the gallery, their warning shouts echoing and re-echoing in the passage. Amran raced towards the wall where the others sheltered, yelling, 'take cover!' He threw himself headlong down behind a fallen strut. Fifty yards behind them the gallery exploded, throwing up the by now almost familiar chunks of stone, coal and splintered wood. 'The gallery is blocked,' Amran spoke, scrambling to his feet.

Darit's terrified voice called, 'Ariel's been hit!'

They found Cohen slumped on the ground, clutching at his stomach. 'It seems that the Nazis have got me in the end,' he muttered, trying to smile. He did not remember having blacked out, but suddenly he found himself staring up at Harari's anxious face, smudged with soot and mud. He wanted to rise, but for some reason his legs would

193

not support him. His overalls were ripped open and covered with blood. Darit was dabbing carefully at his wounds.

Ariel coughed, tasting blood in his mouth, and suddenly felt incredibly weak, although his mind was still clear. He saw his wife Sarah and son Shmuel very vividly; they were all sitting around the table, which had been set for *Hanukkah*. Shmuel was reciting a *broche*.

No pain, only a pleasantly lethargic sensation. So this is what it is like . . . the process of dying, he thought. How long would it take to lose consciousness.

He wanted desperately to remain alert.

Those Goddamned Nazis . . .

Darit had now bandaged his wounds. But Ariel knew he was beyond help. His legs were numb and lifeless, and his voice too now failed him. Hadar and Jorv were still working on the wall.

The pursuers were still working on the last obstacle.

Out of earshot, Hadar asked Darit, 'how is he?'

'Bad,' she answered in a choked voice. Hadar could see that she was fighting back her sobs. 'His abdomen and right lung are perforated. His spine is smashed. Ariel is paralysed from the waist down.'

'God!' Jorv groaned. 'We can't possibly carry him.'

'I don't think he has more than fifteen minutes to live. I cannot stop the haemorrhaging.'

Amran's pick punched a hole in the brickwork and drew a sharp hissing sound like blowing steam. He felt a gust of escaping pressure in his face.

'Methane!' he yelled with desperate urgency. 'Put the masks on!'

They donned their masks and went to assist Ariel and Goldman.

'Move very carefully,' Ariel whispered. 'Don't make any sparks.'

Taking up their spare copper picks, Harari and Amran resumed the work. The bricks cracked and splintered, crashing into the hollow, and the gap quickly widened.

Even Goldman assisted while Darit tried to comfort Ariel, who turned slowly and touched her hand. He then gestured at a box of matches which Jorv had used to light the dynamite fuses. Thinking that Ariel wanted to safeguard it against a freak accident, Darit handed the box to him, then turned her attention to the hole in the wall.

Ariel's fist clenched over the matches. The deep rumbling of rolling boulders and the sound of crashing timber told him that the pursuers were getting close. Then someone in the distant gloom shouted a warning and all activity stopped.

'They've had a whiff of the gas,' Ariel commented, his mouth beneath the mask widening in gleeful satisfaction. There would be no more shooting in the gallery. He wanted to laugh, to holler his head off at the striving enemy, now deprived of guns and grenades.

Guns were useless in the gas-filled gallery.

The minutes ticked by and he prayed to God to keep him alert for a few more minutes, the time his companions needed to reach a safe distance. He knew he would never get through that hole back to freedom, but he was resolved to protect his friends.

Ariel Cohen willed himself back to full consciousness. Never would he have imagined that he could command so much will. His legs and feet were cold and senseless, as if his body ended just below his navel.

He smiled to himself. Legs? What did he need them for? He wouldn't be using his legs any more. His hands and fingers moved readily enough, and they were all he needed.

He rallied himself.

A few more minutes . . .

He must remain strong. He wanted to see his ancient enemies face to face in the moment of death.

Their death!

The last bricks dropped down and the way to the West German side was open. Harari gestured to Amran, who nodded. Both men went back to Cohen and wanted to gather him up, but Ariel shook his head and shook a pointed finger at the opening. Then, with a bit of wood, he traced on the floor one word, '*GO!*'

Up in the gallery lights flashed and the powerful beams swept the walls. The footfalls of oncoming men could be heard. There was no time to waste. Harari and Jorv exchanged glances. Their eyes spoke of immense sadness. Hadar looked at Darit, who shook her head slowly, as if to say that Ariel could not be moved.

Once more, Cohen pointed weakly at the hole in the wall.

A quick embrace, a kiss on the forehead from Darit, an encouraging squeeze of Harari's hand, a gentle pat from Jorv and a long, grateful look of commiseration from Professor Goldman.

Then the team disappeared through the dark hole.

Ariel relaxed. It was easier than he thought it would be. Their mission had been accomplished, brought to a successful conclusion.

Because of Ariel Cohen, an insignificant citizen of a mighty little nation, a jeweller from Tel-Aviv, a patriot, or perhaps just an idiot . . .

Professor Goldman was important, but there were thousands of Ariel Cohens in Israel. The Soviet missiles bought by the Syrians would never reach Israeli targets. The fighters with the Star of David on their fuselages would remain masters of the sky . . .

His son, Shmuel, would not be shot down by an enemy SAM.

Because of Professor Goldman.

And Ariel Cohen . . .

Shmuel would be proud of him. Sarah would cry a lot, but Major Moshe Pesach would console her. Time would alleviate her sorrow.

Perhaps she would even find another goldsmith to run the workshop.

The STASI would never follow Goldman into the West German section. Not because the communists would hesitate about trespassing. There were no guards on the far side of the wall. No collapsed galleries, either.

No witnesses, no NATO troops.

But he, Ariel Cohen, would prevent them continuing the pursuit.

The flashlights were coming closer. They caught Ariel's slumped form in a dozen beams.

Ariel prayed silent, mustered his ebbing strength.

God was with him.

The group of approaching soldiers froze and gazed at him. East Germans and Russians, led by three high-ranking officers, all clutching their useless weapons, rigid in silence and barely five paces from where Ariel lay, propped against the wall.

With a box of matches in his hand, a cluster of matches held together, ready to strike.

A dozen large, round eyes, showing no emotion at all, gazed fixedly at the matches upon which some quirk of fate had bestowed the destructive power of an atomic bomb.

The 'victors' realised that they had lost.

Someone at the rear uttered a low moan. Two shapes turned and bolted for the gallery, while others began to back away. Only the three senior officers still stared and stood rigidly, as if paralysed. Ariel wanted to know their names. He also wanted to laugh.

The KGB and its East German henchmen, running away from Ariel Cohen, a little Jew from Tel-Aviv.

His companions should be far enough away by now. There were no obstacles on the West German side.

Ariel felt dizzy. The lights in front of him swayed in and out of focus. The time has come, he thought.

His fingers holding the matches tightened and moved, then everything dissolved in a terrific, blinding flash of immense brightness that tore across the galleries and swept everything away in its wake.

DEVIL'S GUARD

George Robert Elford

The brutal and shocking testament of a Nazi mercenary.

This is a first hand account of an unregenerate Nazi who escaped the war crimes trials in Europe after World War II and joined the French Foreign Legion.

Sent to Indochina to fight the Viet Minh, the German battalion shot, bombed, tortured and bayonetted the enemy.

Devil's Guard is one man's personal document of reprisals and counter-reprisals, of criminal violence on both sides, of outrages against humanity, of war at its rawest, cruellest and most gruesome.

NEW ENGLISH LIBRARY

KIZILKAR
Red Snow

George Robert Elford

The enemy, infidel and godless, had invaded his land. Men, women and children had been massacred by the clanking armour and the terrifying whispering death of the helicopter gunships.

But the high mountain valleys, the savage barren hills of Afghanistan were his home. Generations before him had fought off and killed all invaders.

This wilderness of white and grey, of snow and bare rock, would be stained and splashed with the sudden red of Russian blood again and again, at whatever cost. Until the hated, despised enemy, ambushed and harried, stripped, shot and dying of exposure, burned alive in their tanks, gunned down like mad dogs, were driven from his country.

For this was a Holy War and only death awaited the foe.

NEW ENGLISH LIBRARY

THE LONGEST DAY

Cornelius Ryan

June 6, 1944 – D-DAY
One of the most important days in the history of mankind.

THE LONGEST DAY – The story of the people; the men
of the allied forces, the enemy they fought, and the
civilians who were caught up in the bloody confusion of
D-Day – the day the battle began that ended Hitler's
insane gamble to dominate the world.

'THE LONGEST DAY is living history: a terrifying
account of splendid bungling, unavoidable mistakes,
cold-blooded horror – and sublime heroism'
SUNDAY EXPRESS

'The terrifying realism of what war really is. D-Day was
the greatest and most necessary military undertaking in
British or American history, and Mr Ryan's book is
worthy of its theme'
THE OBSERVER

NEW ENGLISH LIBRARY

THE LAST BATTLE

Cornelius Ryan

At 4am on April 16, 1945, the Russian army launched its attack on Berlin, the last stronghold of Hitler's Germany.

The Berliners waited in the bombed rubble of their city caring only to survive in the nightmare world around them.

The Allies had declared Berlin no longer a military objective and the US Ninth Army halted forty-five miles from the city. The Russians who had fought their way from Stalingrad swept on . . .

THE LAST BATTLE is a masterly account of those three weeks of the death throes of the Thousand Year Reich. It follows the fortunes of ordinary men and women, soldiers and civilians, victors and vanquished . . . as Berlin was gutted, its women raped, its people terrorised by an invader driven on by vengeance . . .

NEW ENGLISH LIBRARY

MORE GOOD READING

FROM NEL

GEORGE ROBERT ELFORD

☐	01336 7	Devil's Guard	£2.25
☐	05692 9	Kizilkar	£1.50

IAN HARDING

☐	05584 1	Assault Troop 1: Blood Beach	£1.50
☐	05600 7	Assault Troop 2: Death in the Forest	£1.50
☐	05648 1	Assault Troop 3: Clash on the Rhine	£1.60

JAMES ROUCH

☐	04408 4	Gateway to Hell	£0.95
☐	05029 7	The War Machines	£1.25
☐	04768 7	The Zone 1: Hard Target	£1.00
☐	04769 5	The Zone 2: Blind Fire	£1.00
☐	05057 2	The Zone 4: Sky Strike	£1.25

CORNELIUS RYAN

☐	05462 4	The Last Battle	£2.95
☐	05453 5	The Longest Day	£1.95

All these books are available at your local bookshop or newsagent, or can be ordered direct from the publisher. Just tick the titles you want and fill in the form below.

Prices and availability subject to change without notice.

NEL BOOKS, P.O. Box 11, Falmouth, Cornwall.

Please send cheque or postal order, and allow the following for postage and packing:

U.K. – 55p for one book, plus 22p for the second book, and 14p for each additional book ordered up to a £1.75 maximum.

B.F.P.O. and EIRE – 55p for the first book, plus 22p for the second book, and 14p per copy for the next 7 books, 8p per book thereafter.

OTHER OVERSEAS CUSTOMERS – £1.00 for the first book, plus 25p per copy for each additional book.

Name ....

Address ....

....